"A juicy romp through the mind of an uncertain,
hyperbolic, and delightfully flawed fourteen-year-old girl...
highly recommended."

—*Canadian Review of Materials*

mY LiFe
from
aiR-bras
to Zits

For Biff, with much love.

Also in loving memory of
Aunt Mary Dunlea and Aunt Connie Agius.

Barbara Haworth-Attard

mY LiFe
from
aiR-bras
to Zits

flux™
Woodbury, Minnesota

First U.S. Edition
First Printing, 2009

Originally published as *A Is for Angst* by Harper *Trophy*Canada™, an imprint of HarperCollins Publishers Ltd., 2007

This edition published by Flux, an imprint of Llewellyn Publications

Book design by Steffani Sawyer
Cover design by Ellen Dahl
Cover image © 2008 by Image Source/Jupiter Images

Library of Congress Cataloging-in-Publication Data
Haworth-Attard, Barbara, 1953–
  [A is for angst]
  My life from air-bras to zits / Barbara Haworth-Attard.—1st U.S. ed.
     p. cm.
  Originally pub. in 2007 under title: A is for angst.
  Summary: Desperate to be popular, fourteen-year-old Teresa shares her uncertainties with her old Ken and Barbie dolls as she learns that her mother is pregnant, her grandfather has Alzheimers, and having a boyfriend does not automatically solve all her problems.
  ISBN 978-0-7387-1483-7
  [1. Popularity—Fiction. 2. Peer pressure—Fiction. 3. Self-acceptance—Fiction. 4. Family life—Fiction. 5. Grandparents—Fiction. 6. Interpersonal relations—Fiction. 7. High schools—Fiction. 8. Schools—Fiction.]
I. Title.
  PZ7.H31543My 2009
  [Fic]—dc22
                                    2008041936

Flux
Llewellyn Publications
A Division of Llewellyn Worldwide, Ltd.
2143 Wooddale Drive, Dept. 978-0-7387-1483-7
Woodbury, MN 55125-2989, U.S.A.
www.fluxnow.com

Printed in the United States of America

Also by Barbara Haworth-Attard

Dark of the Moon
The Three Wishbells
TruthSinger
Home Child
Buried Treasure
WyndMagic
Love-Lies-Bleeding
Flying Geese
Irish Chain
Theories of Relativity
Dear Canada: A Trail of Broken Dreams—The Gold Rush
Diary of Harriet Palmer
Forget-Me-Not

Anthologies
A Season of Miracles
Winds Through Time
Beginnings
Up All Night
The Horrors

Short stories have appeared in *Cricket Magazine*
and textbooks.

Acknowledgments

Friends are the people who support us and care for us and love us, warts and all. I'd like to thank Beth Cooper, my friend since high school, who knows way too much about me (and yet, is still my best bud); Judy Ann Sadler for her wonderful hugs; and Maggie Wood, who cheers me on when the going gets rough.

Many thanks also to Scott Treimel, my agent, who makes sense of the muddle.

And as always, love to my husband, Joe.

grade 10: tHe BesT YeAr oF mY LiFe: NOT

Here is how Grade 10 started.

The night before school began, Mom came into my room and found me in bed with Ken. She opened my bedroom door as I nibbled on his neck and Ken was telling me how beautiful I was. I tried to shove him under the covers, but I wasn't quick enough and she saw him, naked—black marker genitalia and all.

"Teresa," Mom said. "Why are you sleeping with a doll?" She walked over and picked him up, staring at the black splotches on his you-know-what. "And why have you drawn on him?"

I snatched him back.

Real Reason: I was sleeping with Ken because I was rehearsing what it would be like to be in bed with a boy, in case I ever run into that situation. Not that I have a boyfriend, and I'm not a girl who wants to sleep with a boy until she's way older anyway, but...

Motto No. 1: Always be prepared.

So I had resurrected my Ken doll from the bottom of the closet—and found that cute top I'd been searching eons for. I'd drawn the genitalia because, well, doesn't even Ken deserve private parts? I mean, that smooth plastic mound between his legs has always sort of freaked me out. But I couldn't very well tell Mom that!

Reason For Mom: "Uh...I was feeling a little down and I wanted some company."

ACK! It sounded pathetic to my own ears. I tried to look sad and vulnerable and it was partly true, since I was feeling a little depressed. Which was perfectly understandable. How would you feel if you knew deep down that your Ken doll preferred Barbie, with her big plastic boobs, to you? Obviously he didn't *tell* me that, but I'm pretty sure he does. Seems all boys do. Prefer big boobs, I mean, though not necessarily plastic ones. However, some boys don't seem to mind those either—plastic fake boobs. Confused? Welcome to my life.

Last year in ninth grade, in an attempt to find out

what boys liked in a girl, I pretended I was doing a paper on gender attitudes and asked my older brother, Hugo, what attributes he looked for.

"Brains," he said. "Someone I can discuss politics, religion, and abstinence with."

And then he grinned, and the cream puff he was eating at the time leaked through his teeth like he was foaming at the mouth. Absolutely gross. Seriously, why do girls care so much about these childish imbeciles known as MALES?

"Yes, I like a woman with big brains," he went on. "I mean, brain."

"Women are more than big *brains!*" I told him.

"How would you know? You're a little short in the *brains* department," he sneered.

Okay, that hurt. I've always been a little sensitive about my lack of…ah…*brains.*

"I'm so glad I'm not a guy," I said. "No wonder all you think about are boobs! Because that's what you are. A boob! An idiot!"

Okay, it wasn't a great comeback, but it was the best I could do off the top of my head. Guys are so stupid. Except, of course, AAA: Achingly Adorable Adam. He's brilliant. Well, I've never spoken to him, but he *looks* brilliant.

Problem: The boy of my dreams doesn't even know I'm alive. Yet.

I bet when AAA says he likes big brains he means an intelligent girl, like me. And seriously, how can any girl live up to those Barbie breasts? The dolls should be recalled as contributing to poor self-esteem in females. My own Barbie, though, sits on my dresser, a reminder of my childhood days when life was all sunshine and flowers. At least that's how I fondly remember them. Since I hit twelve, it's been more rain than sun.

But back to the matter at hand. Mom was still standing in my bedroom, eyebrows raised expectantly.

"A black marker must have leaked in the closet," I said. I tried to erase the marker with my thumb and then realized I was rubbing my plastic doll's crotch in front of my mom, so I stopped.

"It made an interesting pattern, don't you think?" I continued.

Motto No. 2: Do not abandon a sinking ship. Hang in there until the last mast is under water. You might actually survive.

"Imagine, Mom, if it had been in the shape of the Virgin Mary. We would have people lining up outside our door to see Ken's privates. We could charge them and make a fortune, except I don't know if it is morally right to charge people to look at a religious icon."

"Teresa, dear. Do you want to talk to *someone*?" Mother interrupted.

I made a list of *someones* in my mind.

Someones:
1. Dad—too awkward.
2. Dad's mom, Grandma T—too proper.
3. Mom's parents, Nanna P or Nannu P—hot Latin blood, so a possibility, but way too old.
4. Hugo—I just threw him in for a laugh. Like I'd ever talk to that jerk.
5. Sophia, my older sister—if it wasn't about her upcoming wedding, she didn't care.
6. Father Bernie—did I do something morally wrong?
7. Biff, best friend—ah. Someone.

"I'll talk to Biff," I said.

"I don't mean Elizabeth," Mom said. "I mean *someone* who knows what you are going through, can help you make sense of your emotions. Puberty is a difficult time."

Omigawd! (Please note: not blasphemy if spelled this way.) She meant SHRINK! Ever since Mom took Psychology 101 at night school, she's been dying for someone in the house to have a problem so she could see how a real shrink works. And I had just given her the perfect opportunity.

"No. Mom, I'm fine. Really, I'm fine." I grinned from ear to ear. See? No one could smile that wide if they weren't fine.

I yawned and tossed Ken into the corner of my bedroom. "I'm real tired, Mom. And school starts tomorrow. I'll need to get some sleep if I'm to be fresh."

Education comes first with Mom and Dad. They are

always sending us to bed at incredibly early hours so we'll be "fresh for school."

"As long as you're sure." Mom hesitated at the door.

"Yep. Absolutely A-OK here. Can you close the light, please?" Nannu P always says that. His English gets mixed up at times. I made a show of burrowing under my covers.

Mom flicked off the light and left.

After a few minutes I got out of bed and picked Ken up from the floor. I spat on his you-know-what and wiped the marker off with a tissue—yes, it was weird for me, too—and put him on the dresser beside Barbie.

"You'd better do some quick talking," I told him. "You cheated on Barbie."

I started to climb into bed, then crawled back out and pointed to Barbie's chest. "And those aren't real, you know. Implants," I told Ken.

And I went to bed feeling quite content because Barbie might have big plastic boobs, but I was THE OTHER WOMAN.

a is For Angst

The first day of tenth grade, and what do I have? A Volcanic Eruption in the middle of my forehead! I've definitely ticked off the Higher Power! (HP) But giving me a pimple on the very first day of school? That's just mean. Maybe this is one of those times sent to try us that Grandma T is always going on about. She says you go into a fire and come out wearing steel armor or something like that. Weird, I know, but remember, it is Grandma T's saying, not mine.

There is only one person who can help me here—other than the HP—and that person is my best friend, Biff.

E-mail
7:00 a.m.
To: Biff
From: T

Subject: URGENT! Volcanic Eruption!

Biff! R U THERE?
EMERGENCY!
Huge zit on forehead. Help!
T

I sent the message off, fingers crossed that Biff would be online. She's smart. Really smart. She wants to be an anthropologist when she graduates. And, no, that's not the study of headgear on deer (okay, I admit, that's what I thought at first too).

From the Internet, the source of all wisdom:

> *Internet Research:* Anthropology is the scientific and humanistic study of man's present and past biological, linguistic, social, and cultural variations.

Say that five times fast!

My Definition: The study of why humans are weird.

The deer headgear person would be an *antler*pologist.

Hugo burst into the living room, tipped me off the chair and planted himself in front of the computer.

"Hey! I was using that," I yelled.

"Not anymore," he said.

I tried to tip *him* off the chair, but couldn't. When did he get so big? Since he'd turned sixteen, everything about Hugo was huge. Feet, hands, arms, mouth—oh yeah, that mouth! He was so LOUD. Since his voice deepened, everything he says BOOMS out. There was just one thing I could do to remove him.

"MOM!" I shouted. "HUGO HIT ME!"

Mom hates violence in any form.

"NO I DIDN'T!" Hugo roared, making my ears ring. "I TIPPED HER."

Mom came into the room and leaned against the wall, looking pale. "Stop it. Both of you! I don't care who hit or tipped. You know the rule. No computer before school."

"It's an emergency, Mom. I have a humongous zit." I swept dark, curly hair from my forehead so she could see the eruption. "And I'm waiting for Biff to get back to me about what I should do."

"I just need to check where the guys are meeting before school," Hugo boomed at the same time.

"Turn it off. Now!" Mom yelled.

I stared at her in surprise. This was very unlike Mom. Her "Parenting Your Teen" course had taught her to *listen* to her children. Listen to the words, but *hear* what they are really saying. It is actually quite annoying having her *hear* me. Her face becomes intense and concerned, her head nods sympathetically, and then, after I say something, she says, "So, what I'm hearing you say is ... " and she repeats exactly what I've just said! Like an echo bouncing off the walls. Very annoying! But not today. Today, she just yelled at us. If I hadn't been so worried about my pimple, I might have been worried about her.

"But Mom," I wailed, "I can't go to school looking like this. I'm disfigured!"

"Teresa, you have a tiny red mark on your forehead. All teenagers have red marks on their faces. Put your hair back over it and go and get dressed. Both of you. You're going to be late the first day of school!"

Hugo and I suddenly looked at each other. *The bathroom.*

We sprinted toward the stairs, but his legs—how did he get so BIG in one summer?—took them two at a time, leaving me far behind. As I reached the bathroom door, I heard the *click* of the lock. Crapola! Now I'd be rushed to get ready, and everyone knows the first day of school requires a ton of preparation time.

I was standing in the hall, fuming, when I noticed Sophia's bedroom door slightly open. She'd already left for work at the insurance company. Maybe she had something I could use to cover my zit.

I tiptoed into Sophia's bedroom, arms stiff at my side. My sister has an uncanny ability to know when someone has been in her room. Being careful not to touch anything, I looked over her dresser, and eureka! Found what I was looking for—a tube of concealer cream. I slid it into my PJ pocket and crept out of the bedroom, leaving the door open exactly the width Sophia had left it earlier. She'd never know I'd been there.

In my own bedroom, I looked at the clothes laid out on my chair. Biff and I had devoted the entire month of August to our first-day-back-to-school look. Well, it would be more accurate to say that I had agonized over it, but Biff had worried right along with me like the best friend she is. We'd studied fashion magazines, watched Fashion Television, checked out a lot of stores, and I had made a list—that's my specialty, lists—of which stores had the best tops and which ones had the best bottoms. Then we'd entered the lists into the computer, cross-referenced them, decided which pair of jeans would go best with which top and purchased them. It went great, except now I hated my outfit. It was all wrong! A zit and the wrong clothes. Could this day get any worse?

I pulled open dresser drawers and began to toss tops onto my bed. If I didn't find the exactly perfect ensemble I'd be destined to the ranks of a Sub-Normal on my very first day of school!

The School Class System

Okay. This is important, vital information, without which a girl can mess up her entire high school experience and ultimately, her life. Teenage society is divided into three classes of people.

Normals (N)

The ordinary kids—like me. We are careful to do nothing to stand out. We talk softly and laugh at the right time—but not a full, head-thrown-back belly laugh that might draw attention to us. We wear neutral clothes that blend in well with the institutional walls (jeans, khaki, beige), and we give up prime seats at the back of the classroom or the cafeteria to the Above-Normals.

Above-Normals (AN)

The Above-Normals are a blessed group. The girls have perfect breasts, white teeth, shiny hair, BOYFRIENDS, their own table in the cafeteria, and always—always—the right clothes. I just don't get the clothes thing. How do they know about fashion trends before the rest of the world? I watch Fashion Television and I read fashion magazines while standing in grocery store lines, but I never get it right.

Are they consulted by fashion designers? "What would you darling ANs like to wear this year?" How do they know that one day it is okay to wear a matching sweater set, but if I wear one the next day their eyes sweep over me with scorn, because they've gone on to pastel T-shirts?

The AN boys are cute, and into sports, sports, sports, and always, always sit with the AN girls in the cafeteria or the sports bleachers. They have lots of money to throw around, some have CARS and most have GIRLFRIENDS.

And then we come to the last group:

Sub-Normals (SN)

I live in absolute terror of becoming a Sub-Normal. ANs never have this particular worry, because SNs are two levels below them. ANs couldn't possibly fall that far unless they did something drastic. On the other hand, it doesn't take much for an N to become an SN: a volcanic pimple on your forehead could do it. Or the wrong clothes!

SNs are distinctive for their stooped shoulders, their backs hugging the wall, and their cringing whenever an AN passes. An SN can never tell if he or she will be thrown against a locker or have his or her school books knocked to the floor. Mind you, an N can never push an SN around—only an AN can. I mean it's not a totally disordered society, there are rules.

I know I should stand up for the injustice of it all, the school class system, blah, blah, blah, but hey, I didn't make the rules.

Now here's the odd thing: Biff isn't anything. She speaks to ANs and Ns and SNs alike. She doesn't care, and that throws everyone off. I mean, she's a teenager. She's supposed to care. But she's an aberration (long word, look it up—I had to): too blonde (natural BTW) to be SN, too brainy to be AN, plus she wears glasses and ANs never wear glasses, except designer sunglasses. Everyone figures she's in the others' group, when she's actually in none at all. It's an absolutely brilliant strategy.

Biff finds the class system in our school fascinating, and she is writing a paper on it that she hopes to have published in *Anthropology Weekly*, or whatever that science magazine is that she reads. Sometimes the way she looks at me makes me wonder if she's using *me* as a case study. I asked her once and she told me no, of course not, but I still feel under the microscope at times.

Just as an aside, Achingly Adorable Adam is in his own Above-Above-Normal group.

The bathroom door opened and Hugo pushed out past me, wrapping a wet towel around my head.

"Jerk," I yelled as I peeled it off my face and tossed it in the dirty clothes hamper.

"Double jerk," I muttered as I looked in the sink.

Lumps of toothpaste and tiny hairs from Hugo's shaver clogged the drain. And he'd left the toilet seat up.

Note to the Unwary: If you live in a house with a male, or if you visit someone who has a brother, look before you sit! Very important if you do not want to find your butt floating in the toilet.

I slammed the toilet seat down. Hugo had taken so long in the bathroom that I only had time for a quick shower. Which meant I'd have to leave for school with my hair wet. And that meant a serious case of frizz!

"Mom," I shouted through the door, "we need another bathroom. I can't believe you expect us all to use just one."

We have a powder room downstairs, but it only has a sink and toilet, which I will be the first to admit comes in handy at times.

"Teresa, just hurry up. I need that bathroom to get ready for work."

"If we had another one, you could be in it, while I'm in here."

"Teresa!" Mom's voice held a warning.

"Well, could we just get rid of Hugo, then?" I turned the faucet on, so I never did hear her reply.

While I showered, I walked through the rooms of our house in my mind. We live in a big city, Toronto, in a semi-detached. That's two houses attached with one wall between them, for those not in the know. Most of the houses on our street are identical semis: brick porch, tiny front yard, no garage, just an asphalt driveway. It's a middle-aged neighborhood with a few large trees.

Traits of a Middle-Aged Neighborhood: Not spanking brand-new like those cool houses on the outskirts of the city. Dad calls those suburban ghettos, but I think they're wonderful. Nor does a middle-aged neighborhood have gracious old mansions with huge yards and lots of trees. Rich people live in those. We've just got boring, thirty-year-old houses with absolutely no distinctive features.

Don't even get me started on our neighbors in the other half, the Middletons. They have twin six-year-old boys, Daniel and Denton, a.k.a. D and D, Destroy and Demolish. We hear them all day long through the attached wall. I babysit them and have serious concerns, as in, *they might be serial killers in the making.*

We have three bedrooms upstairs: Mom and Dad's, Sophia's, and mine. Hugo has a bedroom in the basement that Dad built him. What happened is that Sophia and I shared a room until two years ago, but then she became

Miss Wedding Psycho and Mom said she couldn't take our fighting anymore, so Dad built the extra room downstairs. I think it's really to keep Hugo separated from the rest of us normal people. Sophia is getting married in February.

I bent my head and dried my hair with a towel. All the blood must have rushed to my brain and made me extra smart, because I suddenly had an absolutely fabuloso idea! After Sophia leaves, Dad could knock out the wall between Sophia's and my bedrooms, and I could have my very own ensuite bathroom! Like the ones in those *suburban ghetto* houses. Whirlpool tub, scented candles. Wait until Biff heard about my new bathroom! Dad, Mom, and Hugo could use the other one.

Mental Note to Self: Present Dad with bathroom plan.

Thanks to Hugo, I was late, so I took the porch stairs in a single leap and fell flat on my face over a bike in the middle of our sidewalk. D and D! They leave stuff everywhere. That's one of the traits of a serial killer personality: disregard for other people. I rubbed at the grass stains on the knees of my new jeans, then sprinted to the corner.

Biff lives two blocks over from me, in a house that isn't attached to anything other than a garage. We always meet at the intersection of our two streets, Hincks (Biff's) and Jones (mine.) A warm rush of gratitude (I would say love but that makes me sound like a lesbian) filled me when I saw Biff waiting for me. My best friend.

b is For Boobs
(a.k.a. Breasts and idiots)
AnD Best FrieNDS

Best friends are special. Here is why:

Best Friend Traits:
1. Always waits for you even if it means they will be late themselves.
2. Likes you even when you're PMS-ing.
3. Dances to the same music as you do. (Sometimes they dance better, but they never point that out.)
4. Sticks up for you even when you're wrong. (Though I seldom am.)
5. Giggles insanely at your non-funny jokes.
6. Says you look fabuloso even if you have zits on your face and a case of hair frizz.
7. Understands she comes in second to a boyfriend (and bears no ill will about it).

8. And never, ever, ever steals your boyfriend. (As neither of us has ever had a boyfriend, we haven't tested those last two traits yet.)

"You're not wearing the top we picked out," Biff said.

"I decided it was all wrong."

"Oh."

"What do you mean, 'Oh'?" I asked anxiously. "Do you mean, 'Oh' as in 'You made a big mistake'? Or do you mean, 'Oh you look great'? What? Tell me? Should I go change?" I'm always a little excitable on the first day of school. It's because of my birthday. I was born on December 31st. Yep. New Year's Eve. So I am always the youngest person in my class (that's how it works here in Canada). If I had been born a few hours later, on New Year's Day, I'd be the oldest person in my grade. As the youngest, I'm always trying to compensate for that, which makes me excitable.

"I mean, 'Oh, you didn't wear the top we picked out.' That's all. You don't have time to change. You look just fine," Biff said.

"Fine?!!??" Fine was the kiss of death! When people say *fine*, they really mean horrible. I can't believe I'm going to school on the first day looking FINE.

"The top is good," Biff assured me.

I studied her clothes. "You're wearing what we picked out," I said.

"I thought that was the point of the entire month of August devoted to first-day-back-to-school look," Biff said. "Though," she added, "this behavior you are exhibiting is an interesting insight into the insecurities of teenagers. I wonder if it's just girls who experience this insecurity? Did Hugo choose special first-day clothing?"

"How would I know?" I said. Like I'd ever noticed what Hugo wore. "You look really great," I added, slightly grudgingly. (Best friends can be slightly grudging and get away with it.) Biff did look absolutely fabuloso as per usual, except for one thing.

"When are you going to get contact lenses?" I asked.

"Why? I'm perfectly happy with my glasses," she said.

Biff's Glasses: Inch-thick lenses and black frames.

"Besides," she continued, "contact lenses are a ploy by conglomerate companies preying on people's insecurities to make loads of money."

I bet she's got a phobia about stuff going into her eyes. I'd heard about that.

"Are you afraid to put them in?" I asked, trying to be all empathetic and kind.

"Did you get the e-mail I sent back to you?" she said, ignoring my question.

I grimaced. "Hugo kicked me off the computer, then Mom kicked us both off."

Biff studied my face. "I don't see a zit."

"I used Sophia's concealer," I said. The concealer that I had left in my PJ pocket and had to remember to put back on Sophia's dresser before she discovered it was missing. "But it's a big zit. Huge. I'll probably have a scar."

Biff and I discussed my zit and various treatments until we arrived at school.

The place buzzed with that first-day-of-school … um … buzz. I said hello to a few other Ns, nodded my head respectfully to the ANs, and avoided eye contact with the SNs. Biff smiled on all class levels with equal radiance. My AAA radar was on, but so far, no sign of Adam.

Outside the gym was a list of homerooms with the names of the students in them. I gave a squeal of delight when I saw that Biff and I were in the same homeroom, with Monsieur Papineau. I'd had him last year for French and he was okay. Tall and stick-thin with a thatch of red hair, he looked like a pencil with an eraser on the end. He always wore a shirt and tie, unlike some of the other teachers who wore T-shirts and jeans so they'd look cool. Like Miss Cook, my soon-to-be gym teacher. First of all, she wore TTPs. (Too Tight Pants, for the uninformed.) I mean, when you turn twenty-five, you really should give up trying to look young. M. Papineau didn't try to look cool, so therefore, he *was* cool.

Our homeroom was made up largely of Ns, a handful of ANs (you'd think being in the majority, the Ns could take them on, but it just doesn't work that way), and a scattering of SNs—including—Omigawd! (not blasphemy, remember?)—Phillip White! What was he doing here? I ducked my head and hid behind Biff until we found seats, then I stacked up my books and crouched behind them. Why, you may ask?

A Little Background Information

Before the Middletons, Phillip's family was our next-door neighbor for ten years. And he and I had been best friends for seven of them. He was clumsy and awkward, brainy, and just plain geeky, but I could ignore that because he went along willingly with any incredible adventure idea I came up with. But in fifth grade I noticed how the other kids began to either ignore him or target him. Now here's a question for anthropologist Biff: How do kids, myself included, instinctively know when someone is different? That they're not cool? How do we instantly know the class status of every kid? Is it just humans who do this or do, say, penguins have Ns, ANs, and SNs?

Fantasy: I am immune to peer pressure and am friends with everyone.

Truth: I have no immunity. I do what everyone else does. That's just THE WAY IT IS. There are winners and there are losers, and there are others, like me, desperately treading water in the middle. Accept it. It'll never change.

Oddly, Phillip himself knew he was "different." So in fifth grade we had a sort of unspoken agreement that he'd not talk to me at school, but we'd be friends at home. See, even he accepted that's just THE WAY IT IS. The boys used to call him a name, not a nice one, but I couldn't remember what it was. Phillip's family moved halfway through seventh grade.

I took a peek from behind my books. Phillip had sure grown. He was tall and skinny with a huge Adam's apple bobbing up and down his throat. His forehead was too high, his nose—gosh, it was like a beak. Some ugly ducklings turn into beautiful swans. Unfortunately, Phillip had blossomed into a geeky flamingo!

I surfaced a second time to do a quick clothing check and was relieved to see my top was fine. In fact, one of the ANs was wearing one quite similar. Or was that a bad thing? Maybe she'd be mad I'd worn the same top! Rats! I also noticed she filled hers out better than I did. Double rats!

M. Papineau did the attendance, and I mumbled "Here" when he called my name, then quickly slouched back in my seat. Five minutes were wasted on one of the AN girls trying to make M. Papineau pronounce her name correctly ("It's Ash*la-a-y*, not Ash*lee*"). I mean, really; Ashlee is way too common for an AN who has her very own girl gang—the Glams.

The Glams:

Melanie: pretty with long brown hair, but very dumb.
Stephanie: plain looking but the brains of the bunch, which isn't saying much, and the "yes" girl.

Note to the Uninformed: "Yes" people agree with everything another person says.

Kara: big brains. Rumor has it she lets guys squeeze her brains after she chugs a few beers. And I'm not just passing that rumor on because I have brains-envy.

Brains/Boobs Discussion: Boys love them, and girls want them because boys love them. That's it. Discussion over.

Every school has a girl like Ash*la-a-y* . What is it that lets one person have all the power? How come she gets minions (another long word to look up) to do her bidding? And what about the others who follow her like brainless zombies just to be popular? How pathetic is that?

Truth No. 1: I'd be a brainless zombie in a minute if I could get into the Glams.
Truth No. 2: I really am that shallow.

We filled out forms listing next-of-kin, health insurance details, and boring stuff like that for an hour. Then M. Papineau gave us our locker locations and handed out our class schedules. Because it was the first day, we did a ten-minute class rotation to meet our teachers and get supply lists, which we had to have filled by the next day. Thus, the shortened classes so we could get that done.

My Grade 10 Courses First Semester:

English: Mrs. Cockburn. Guys snicker at her name all the time, even though she's ancient—at least thirty—and it's pronounced Co-burn, not the other rude way.

Math: Mr. Bolton. He has a lame moustache and

wears the same red sweater every day, but don't tell him! He's mean and will fail you just for fun. *His* fun.

History (snooze time): Mr. Timber. He's so enthusiastic about history that even if the class didn't show up one day, he would talk about old stuff to empty desks.

Last class of the day, Physical Education/Health Class: Miss Cook of the TTPs. She has a whistle permanently installed around her neck. I bet she even uses it outside of school. There are few things I hate more than Physical Education. Nope, I'll amend that. There's nothing I hate more than Physical Education. I'm okay with exercising, but not as a team sport. I'm more an individual type of exerciser. But it's a required credit so I have to take it.

Biff and I were in three classes together, but because she's so smart—above-normal (little joke)—she gets to take Grade 11 Biology instead of sweaty gym as her last class of the day. We sadly parted ways for ten minutes, but not before I made her promise to meet me at the school doors at dismissal. Walking alone *to* school is forgivable. I mean, early in the morning you could use the excuse of sleeping in or missing a bus, but at the end of the day, well, there are just no excuses for being on your own, unless you are an SN. Then it's expected that you'll be on your own.

After hearing Miss Cook expound on the *virtues of*

exercise (boring), and *the importance of good sex education* (marginally interesting), I found my locker, dumped my books, and headed to the exit doors. And there was Biff, waiting for me like the best friend she is. Again, I felt that rush of love/gratitude. Is this something I should be worried about? Could I like AAA—and still be a lesbian? Maybe I am bi!

I edged past the Glams, who were blocking the steps as they compared summer tan lines, and came to an abrupt stop. There, in the middle of the ANs, was Hugo! Laughing. A big, head-thrown-back laugh. I felt like I'd run into a brick wall. I couldn't breathe. My brother was an AN!

They say the family is always the last to know. You live in such close proximity to a person that you miss the clues, or else you just don't want to believe what is right under your nose—the constant phone calls from girls all summer, the female cashiers smiling at him in the grocery store, friends with cars dropping by the house.

I gripped Biff's arm. "Hugo's an AN!"

"It's fascinating," Biff said. She was busy writing in her notebook.

"I never knew."

"They say the family is always the last to know," Biff said.

(Can you see why we're best friends?)

"But shouldn't I automatically be an AN, then?" I asked. "He is my brother."

"I don't think it's a hereditary position," Biff said. "You probably have to become one on your own merits."

"What merits? I mean, it's Hugo!"

"His inclusion is not as large an anomaly as it seems," Biff said. "He does play on the school hockey team and ... " She peered at him over the top of her glasses. "Over the summer he has become, well, hot!"

"Hot?" Puh-leeze. "Biff! That is so gross. How could you say such a thing?"

Biff stuffed her notebook and pen into her backpack. "I wasn't aware of his status last year, but the first year of high school is one of turmoil and perhaps we missed it. Or perhaps his status changed over the summer. And as I said, he has improved physically. The best part of all this is that I can study Hugo through you. A close-up of an AN interacting with an N."

I wasn't sure I liked that idea.

"So," Biff went on, "do you have a list of what you need?"

"Huh?" I was still thinking about Biff studying Hugo "interacting" with me. She was an only child so she was unaware of life with siblings. We argue, hurl insults, ruin each other's lives, but one thing we don't do is interact.

"School supply list?" Biff asked.

"Oh, I certainly do," I said.

During Miss Cook's speech I had written a list of school supplies, along with which store each item could be purchased at, then cross-referenced those with the mall layout to maximize our shopping time. Anthropology may be Biff's thing, but lists and organization are mine.

"Should we go to the mall, then?"

"I need to call Mom and let her know I'm going," I said. "Can I borrow your cell phone?"

It is so embarrassing to have to ask to borrow Biff's phone. I mean, everyone has a cell phone—everyone, that is, except me. Mom doesn't believe in kids having cell phones.

Mom's Argument: Cell phones cause brain damage from all those radioactive waves going right through your ear into your brain.

Biff handed me her cell phone.

" ... it's just that my battery is dead," I said loudly, and I punched in Mom's work number. "Such a pain."

I didn't want people to know I was so uncool that I didn't have a cell phone.

Biff rolled her eyes. "Does Hugo have a phone?"

"No," I said. "But he has the brain damage, so everyone thinks he does."

3

C is For CoNDimeNts
(a.k.a. Condoms)

I spread my school supplies over the kitchen table: binders, pens, lined paper, a calculator, and a red-striped T-shirt. This is the best part about going back to school—new stuff—bought with Mom and Dad's money. Seeing it laid out on the table was like seeing new possibilities. The pages were blank, the binders wrapped in plastic, the pens still had caps, and the T-shirt was going to make me look great. Seeing that stuff, it was easy to believe that I was new too, this year. The new Teresa who had great clothes, tons of friends—including an almost BOYFRIEND named Adam—and a cell phone.

Mom and Sophia sat at the other end of the table going over wedding plans for the gazillionth time.

"You know we're not made of money," Mom said. "Do we really need a crystal bowl for every wedding guest?"

"It's a tradition lately for the bride to give each of her guests a gift," Sophia told her. "But if you want me to go cheap, I suppose I could wrap up a few hard candies in plastic sandwich bags."

"I'm sure there's a middle ground," Mom murmured.

"How can it be tradition when it's a new idea?" I said. "It takes years for something to become tradition."

"And you should keep your mouth shut," Sophia snapped back.

Really, she has become quite a b-t-h (you can fill in the spaces) since she became a bride-to-be. Anthony (the groom, who is really quite yummy-looking for an older guy!) is in for quite a shock once he sees the REAL Sophia. It's no coincidence that "bride" and "b-t-h" both start with *B*, have five letters, and are single-syllable words.

"Why did you buy the T-shirt?" Mom asked. She unfolded the red shirt.

Rats! My mouth had drawn attention to myself. "You told me to go and buy school supplies," I reminded her. "I'll be wearing it to school; thus, it comes under the heading of school supplies," I finished grandly.

Mom raised her eyebrows. "That's stretching the definition rather a bit." She examined the shirt. "And this is a rather low neckline."

"I know." I grabbed the T-shirt out of her hands. "That's what makes it so great. It accents my boobs."

Sophia snorted. "What boobs?"

"Breasts," Mom corrected us. Mom says only women with no self-esteem call them *boobs*. Empowered women have *breasts*. I ducked into the bathroom and pulled on the T-shirt. I stuck out my BREASTS and admired myself a moment, then went back into the kitchen.

"See?" I strutted around the room, turning sideways so they could get a look at my new womanly profile. Sophia began to laugh.

Mom looked distressed. "Teresa, dear," she said. "You are much more than your breasts. I really worry about your self-image."

I tore back into the bathroom and examined my chest in the mirror. In the harsh light of reality (a.k.a. Sophia's laughter), I could see that the T-shirt was awful. My collar bone jutted out—the only thing that did BTW! Reality sucks.

I pulled the T-shirt over my head and flung it onto the kitchen table, and then grabbed my sweater.

Mom picked up the top and turned it right side out.

"I know at this time in your life ... " she began.

I rudely interrupted. "Mom, boys like big boobs." Upset, I shoved my head through the sleeve instead of the neck of my sweater and nearly suffocated. Sophia rescued me and straightened the sweater.

"You shouldn't define yourself by what boys like," Mom went on.

Sophia rolled her eyes at me behind Mom's back. For once we were in agreement. *Of course* we should define ourselves by what boys like. We're *girls* and that's what girls do.

Dad wandered into the room and grabbed a pop from the fridge. "What's going on in here?" he asked. He took in the bride magazines scattered across the table. His voice rose in alarm. "Not more wedding stuff? I'm not made of money, you know."

"So Mother has already informed me," Sophia said icily. "Fine, if you want me to have the worst wedding ever, we could go to the donut shop for the reception. That should keep costs down."

"The coffee's good there," Dad commented.

Sophia glared at him.

"We're discussing Teresa's breasts and her self-image," Mom said.

Note To Mothers Everywhere: Do Not Discuss Daughter's Emerging Womanhood with Father! Yuck!

I nearly died on the spot. So did Dad. He glanced at my chest, then my face, and his eyes bulged with terror.

"Um ... yeah ... well." He backed out of the room. "Hugo," he called. "Get down here. We ... we need to go outside and play a little one-on-one." Man stuff to counteract embarrassing female stuff. Dad was really desperate.

Facts You Should Know About My Dad:
1. He hates outside. Anywhere outside.
2. He hates sports. Playing them. He doesn't mind watching them.
3. He hates people—speaking to them or having them speak to him, that is.

"Where did you get that T-shirt?" Sophia asked.

"At In Stitches, at the mall."

A tear escaped my eye and ran down my cheek. "Biff lied to me. She said it looked good."

"No she didn't," Sophia said. "There's the *store look*, and then there's the *home look*. At the store, the salespeople tell you that everything you try on looks great, and you believe them. The light in the fitting rooms is poor. And with that music blaring, you can't think clearly. You could put on a burlap bag and think you look wonderful. So you buy it, bring it home, try it on, and you realize it's just a burlap bag. That's the *home look*. That's why you make sure anything you buy can be returned."

She stood up. "Mom, T and I are going to the mall for a bit. Can I have the car?"

"It's a school night," Mom protested. "Teresa needs her sleep so she can be fresh for tomorrow."

"School doesn't actually start until the second week. The first week is just for socializing. We're going to take the top back," Sophia said.

Mom slowly turned over the car keys. "Well, don't be late."

Sophia swept me out of the door and into the car. "We

are going where no mother and daughter have gone before, at least together," she said.

. . . . .

At the mall, Sophia strode directly to the In Stitches store and plunked the T-shirt on the counter. "We'd like to return this."

The girl behind the counter examined her nails, then stared at a spot above our heads, looking bored even though she had huge boobs (how can you be bored when you have huge boobs?). That's when I realized that she had on the same top I was returning. What was I thinking?

"Why?" she said coldly.

"It's too small," Sophia said. She flashed her left hand so her diamond glinted. Extra ammunition. (I'm engaged. You?)

"My sister's breasts just fall out of it. It also looks trashy."

The girl glared at Sophia and then eyed me. I jutted out my chest. I could fall out of tops if I wanted to.

T-shirt returned and money in hand, Sophia bombed through the mall and into Prim and Proper Lingerie.

"Let's buy you some boobs," she said. "Oh, I mean, *breasts*. We're empowered women."

I looked curiously around the store. Biff and I had never had the nerve to go into it on our own. Thongs, garter belts, silky black bras, lace teddies. Prim and proper it wasn't. It felt great to be there. Womanly. Adult. I tried for a casual look as I stroked silk boxer shorts—for women!!!

Sophia's fingers flew expertly through the bras on a rack. She pulled one out. "Here, try this on."

I fingered it. It had soft little pouches under the cups. "What is this?"

"Air," Sophia said. "There are little air pouches to raise your breasts. They push you up. It makes you look like you have more. Lots more. Trust me. Go and try it on." She pushed me toward the fitting room.

A few minutes later I was completely agog. She was right! I now had breasts, cleavage, curves. I admired myself in the mirror. I looked … dare I say it? HOT!

"Are you ever coming out?" Sophia asked.

"I can't believe it. It's a miracle. How come I've never seen these before?"

"Because you always go with Mom to get underwear at cut-rate department stores!"

"I want to wear it home," I said. "I'm never wearing this old bra again."

I threw my arms around Sophia when I came out of the fitting room. "Thank you, thank you for bringing me here. I take back every mean thing I ever said to you. I don't have any money right now, but I promise I'll pay you back for it."

Sophia grinned. "You don't have to. It's my gift to you."

I just about crushed her. A new hot bra and I wasn't out any money. Does life get any better than this?

"Do you have one of these bras?" I asked.

Sophia stopped at a table piled high with thongs. "Do I look like I need that bra?"

Good point. She didn't need any help in that area. She'd inherited Mom's full figure. Guys drooled over her.

She sorted through the thongs. "I could do with some more of these."

"You wear those?" I said.

"You know, you really must stop shopping with Mom." She selected five thongs, paid for them, and handed two to me. "There you go. No more panty lines."

I couldn't believe it. I had thongs, too. Wait until Biff heard!

Sophia glanced at her watch, "If we hurry we can hit the bridal shop and you can try on your maid of honor gown."

Okay, if there was one thing I didn't want to do, it was try on my maid of honor gown. It was hideous. Puke green with a pink ribbon that tied under my breasts in the *princess style*—yuck. But Sophia had bought me a bra—which might help the dress—and thongs, so I couldn't in all conscience complain.

I matched Sophia step for step, swinging my bag of thongs down the mall. I noticed guys throwing glances our way. I knew most of them were for her, but maybe some were for me.

"Don't do that," Sophia said.

"What?"

"You're prancing. You're like one of those white show horses."

"The *Lippwhatever*. … stallions?"

"I don't know what they're called. Just stop doing it."

"Guys are looking at you," I said.

"So? Ignore them. They're boobs looking at boobs."

"Is Anthony a boob?" I asked.

Her eyes actually got dreamy. You see that written in books, but this was the first time I'd ever seen it happen for real. It was kind of cool. "No, Anthony is different. He loves me for me."

Yeah, right. He loves those boobs.

"So, do you guys use *condiments*?" I slipped in the question.

I'd always wanted to ask Sophia that, but the opportunity never presented itself. Until now. It wasn't often that Sophia was all warm and fuzzy.

"Condiments?" Sophia stopped and looked in a window at some shoes. "You mean, like ketchup or mustard on hot dogs?"

My Definition of Condiments: Condoms. That word freaks me out. I can't even say it, so I say condiments.

"Uhh … *condiments,* you know, for birth control," I finished in a rush.

I didn't want to know in a nosy *what does my sister do with her boyfriend way* (eww, gross), but as a religious question. (Okay, I was nosy.) The Catholic Church has a very strong stance on using birth control. Don't. Dad says the reason Catholics aren't to use birth control is so that there are lots of new little Catholics being produced.

"I mean, you and Anthony are almost married. And hey, we're all adults here."

"You're not," Sophia said.

"Are you waiting to get married before you have sex?"

"That's none of your business," Sophia replied.

"Well, after you're married and having sex all the time, will you use uh … *condiments*?" Seriously, I can't say condoms. The word will not come out of my mouth. "Or the Pill? Even though Catholics aren't supposed to?"

Sophia stopped walking and grabbed my arm, spinning me around.

"Is someone pressuring you to have sex?"

"No," I said. If only. "I don't even have a boyfriend."

"Good. Then it's none of your business."

And that ended that conversation.

We hit the bridal shop and the dress looked marginally better with my new bra. But even it couldn't change the puke-green color.

• • • • •

On the way home, Sophia suddenly said, "They're not all that you think they are."

"Huh?"

"Large breasts. At times my back aches, I have trouble finding a top that doesn't make me look like a slut and no guy, except Anthony, cares what I have to say or even looks at my face for that matter. Believe me, you're better off the way you are."

I'd never considered that breasts might be a nuisance. I'd always thought big breasts meant you had it made.

"Jugs," I said.

"What?"

"It's another name for breasts."

"Hooters," Sophia said after a minute.

And while we drove home, we made a list of all the names we could think of for breasts.

Breast List
    Breasts
    Boobs
    Hooters
    The Girls
    Bosom
    Bust
    Tits
    Bazoomas
    Jugs

Then just for fun we did a list for penis.

Penis List
    Penis
    Johnson
    Cock
    Willie

Dick
Prick (penis and obnoxious person)
Weiner and Pee Pee (little kids use this)
Woody (that's for when it's ... well, ready for a *condiment*)
Pecker

"Hey, what about Woody Pecker?" I said.
Sophia and I nearly peed ourselves laughing.

4

d is For Diversity

The whole Sophia, Anthony, *condiment*, church thing kept me awake most of the night.

My Diagnosis: I'm analytical.
Mom's Diagnosis (Psychology 101): Obsessive. Getting a thought in your head and examining it every which way until you make yourself crazy.

Back to my analysis. We're Catholic. Every room in our house has a crucifix on the wall or over the doorway. Every room in Nanna and Nannu P's house has a cross, as do all the rooms in my aunts' and uncles' houses. I thought everyone had the same religious decor until I started hanging around with Biff last year. The first day I went to her house, I asked her where the crucifixes and Virgin Mary statues were.

"We're nothing," Biff said.

"Huh?"

"We haven't any religious icons because we don't attend a church, nor are we particularly religious," Biff explained.

My chin dropped to my knees. I knew she wasn't Catholic, but I figured she must at least be Presbyterian or one of those other poor deluded religions that thought they were going to a Heaven that, unfortunately, was strictly reserved for Catholics. But nothing?

It also made me realize what a sheltered life I'd led, thanks to Mom, who'd obviously hand-picked all my friends, first making sure they were Catholic! Even Phillip was Catholic.

"You can't be 'nothing,'" I said. "There's no such thing as 'nothing.'"

"Mom says she is spiritual but doesn't require a building or organized religion to tell her that, and Dad's an atheist. That's someone who doesn't believe in God," she added.

"I know what an atheist is," I said, though I struggled to not let the shock show in my face. I mean, you'd never know to look at Biff's dad that he was an atheist. He's so normal.

Biff is my first real non-Catholic friend. When Sophia started high school, Mom had a tough decision to make. Did she let her kids be bussed to an inner-city Catholic high school, or would they go to the public high school three blocks from our house? She weighed the pros and cons and decided on the nearer, sinful, non-Catholic school. Aunt Grace told Mom we'd all turn out to be heathens. Mom said she wanted us to be exposed to all religions and races so that we'd receive a broader education and understand diversity. Yeah, right. Mom never could stand up to her older sister.

Still, I wasn't sure Mom would want me hanging out with a real heathen, so Biff and I made up a religion for Biff's family.

Biff's Religion: The Fundamental Church of God's Word. (Catchy, huh? My idea.)

But that's as far as we had gotten—a name—when Biff came to my house for the first time and met Mom.

"So, Elizabeth," Mom said, "where do you go to church?"

I saw Biff's lips start to form "nowhere." I jumped in.

"The Fundamental Church of God's Word."

"Pardon?" Mom said.

"That's the name of her church," I said.

"I've never heard of it. Where is it?"

"On the east side of the city," Biff said.

"On a street you don't know," I added for good measure.

I could see Mom looking dubious, so I thought I better make up some realistic church rituals.

"They're snake-handlers," I told her. I'd recently seen

a show on television about churches where people handled snakes and believed God protected them so they couldn't be poisoned by the snake's venom.

"Snake-handlers?"

"Biff doesn't actually handle the snakes," I said. "The pastor does that." The "pastor" part was inspired—we had a priest, non-Catholics had "pastors" or "ministers."

"No, I only handle the arachnids," Biff put in.

Arachnids? Biff had gone too far.

"And they heal people. Faith healing." Damage control. Distract Mom from the spiders.

Mom sank into a chair, stupefied.

"Isn't it great that we can all live in harmony despite our different religions? Diversity, Mom." I pushed Biff out of the kitchen.

"Arachnids?" I poked Biff in the back once we were out of view.

"I thought it would seem even more plausible if I inserted another element," she said.

"There are serpents all over the Bible," I said. "But there aren't any spiders."

"And how would I know what's in the Bible?" she asked.

Hmmm ... good point. "Still," I complained, "I think we had her until the spider part. I don't think she believes us now."

Of course, no one could be as religious as the Maltese people, not even the Pope! Nannu P says that in Malta almost every single day there is a religious celebration of some saint or other. It must be great to get all those holidays from school.

A Little Background Information
Note to the Unwary: My family is as boring as beige paint. Don't read unless you want a good nap.

Mom's Family Tree
My Nannu (that's Maltese for Grandpa) Salvatore Psaila wooed (I love that old-fashioned word) my Nanna (Grandma) Maria in Malta and they got married. They "knew" each other in the biblical sense at least five times because they had five daughters, of which Mom, Fiona, is the youngest. After girl number five, Nannu packed everybody onto a ship and brought them to New York—right past the Statue of Liberty—and to Canada. He said there weren't enough men in Malta for all the girls he was producing and he needed fresh fields if he wasn't going to be stuck with spinsters. All the Psailas are very, very Catholic. All of Malta is very, very Catholic.

Dad's Family Tree
Grandpa Tolliver "wooed" Grandma Ellen and married her in England, and they came to Canada after World War II. Grandma T still has a snobby English accent. My dad, Marshall Frederick Tolliver, who does not have a snobby English accent, was an only child. At one of our famous

family Sunday dinners, Nannu told us why Dad was an only child.

"That woman," Nannu said, referring to Grandma T, "she have one child, and after that, kept her legs crossed for the rest of her life. We didn't have that problem, did we, Maria?"

"Pa!" Mom and Nanna exclaimed in unison. "The children!"

Nannu doesn't like Grandma T because she once called him a barbarian.

Grandpa T died six years ago. I don't really remember him that much.

"Those crossed legs. That's what killed him," Nannu announced at another Sunday dinner.

"Pa! The children!"

Grandma T has done a genealogy chart that shows Dad's side of the family is descended from English royalty. Personally, I don't believe it, because our noses are too stubby and everyone knows royal blood equals big honkers.

Malta
A tiny set of islands off the toe of Italy in the Mediterranean, where every one of the 394,000 people, except for five of them, are Catholic. The country runs itself now, though until 1964 it was under British rule. Maybe that's why Nannu doesn't like Grandma T! Wow! I haven't taken any psychology classes, yet I figured that out. Maybe I'm a natural psychologist. I wonder how much psychologists make to just sit there and listen to people complain?

England

Nothing to say here. Everyone knows England.

My Own Family Tree

Dad met Mom at a dance. He's always telling us how he fell in love with her at first sight, with her warm brown eyes and her black wavy hair, and that she was the most beautiful girl in the room.

So Mom took Dad home to meet her parents. At first the Psailas forbade (isn't that medieval?) them to marry because Dad wasn't Catholic. He was Methodist. It really is very Romeo and Juliet-y because Mom said if she couldn't marry Dad, she would enter a convent. Now Nanna liked the idea of a nun in the family, but she liked the idea of grandchildren more. They only had about a dozen already! So they finally let Mom marry Dad, after Dad promised to let Mom raise us kids as Catholics. So I'm half Maltese and half English and full Catholic.

I have blocked from my mind Mom and Dad "knowing each other"—so let's just say that Sophia, Hugo, and I are all immaculate conceptions and we'll leave it at that.

Mom works in a bank as a teller. About three years ago she began to take night classes to "better" herself.

Translation: "Get out of the house before I go stark raving mad."

These days it is Psychology 101.

Dad owns a construction company. He does not take night classes as he feels he's good enough already and doesn't want to be better. Mom says he has a social phobia.

Along with people, Dad doesn't like nature, either. Anything that's outside the four walls of our house, he hates. He loves inside, especially the couch and the television. He's medium height. A bit of a stomach hangs over his belt; he has skinny chicken legs when he wears shorts, which we do not encourage him to do, brown hair on the sides of his head only, and a shiny dome on top. I think when Mom met him he probably had more hair and looked better.

Siblings

Sophia is twenty-one, has a business diploma, works in an insurance office as a claims adjuster, and is marrying nice Catholic, Maltese Anthony on Valentine's Day. Isn't that just too sweet? Not!

Hugo is sixteen, has big feet, smells, and is dumber than dumb, which is pretty dumb. Not much else to say about him.

Now Me

I'm fifteen—well, on December 31st, so that is close enough to be called fifteen. I have thick, curly, black hair like my mom, but my dad's English hazel eyes and pale coloring. I look like I'm a bit off, like milk just starting to go sour. I'm small on top (my biggest agony)—Grandma T's fault. But my bottom is big—Nanna P's fault!

Mental note to self: Do bum crunches.

I am in tenth grade. As I said, my best friend is Biff, of the blonde hair and blue eyes and Va-Va-Voom figure that I've literally seen guys drool over. Really! Serious saliva strings.

At the moment, I have no idea what career path I'll take. I'm a free spirit, open to anything that doesn't involve a lot of hard work but pays tons of money.

And finally and most importantly, I'm totally in love with AAA—Achingly Adorable Adam—of the spiked black hair, don't-give-a-crap saunter, brown eyes, full lips (smack! kiss!), who is in eleventh grade and doesn't know I'm alive. My goal this year is to make Adam notice me!

e is For ELection
(a.k.a. erection)

My head thumped against the hardwood floor and my eyes flew open.

"Where is it, you little freak?" Sophia howled. She'd yanked me out of bed—sheets, pillows, comforter, and all.

I spat blanket fuzz from my baby cuddle-blankie. Oops, didn't mean to reveal that. (Okay, I have trouble letting go of childhood stuff: my Barbie doll, my blankie, the five-year-old cherry bubblegum that's on the underside of my desk.) I struggled to untangle my legs from the sheets. "What? What are you talking about?"

"My concealer. Where is it? I'm already late for work."

Oh yeah, Sophia's concealer. I'd left it in my PJ pocket. I'd meant to return it but had been so busy showing Barbie my new bra (not Ken, though; he doesn't need to know all women's secrets), I'd forgotten.

"Hang on." I rummaged through yesterday's laundry and fished out her concealer. "Did you have to wake me up so early? I could have slept another twenty minutes."

Sophia snatched the tube out of my hand and headed toward the door. "I don't have time to deal with you right now, but tonight you're dead."

"Oh, nice talk," I said. "Do you speak that way to Anthony?"

She turned back and I jumped onto the bed out of reach. "I had a big zit," I whined. Did I mention that bravery is not my strong point? Besides, Sophia is Tolliver Women Wrestling Champ (TWWC). She can even take Hugo down.

"Better make out your last will and testament." Sophia slammed the door on her way out.

"Yeah, well, I'm not leaving you anything in that will." I can be brave to empty rooms.

The door opened again, and I jumped into my closet and cowered on the floor.

"Get out of my room you, you … *hamar*," I yelled.

"I beg your pardon?" Mom poked her head around the closet door. "We don't call people an ass in this house."

"I was using the donkey definition, not the other," I protested.

Translation: *Hamar*—Maltese for "ass." (Not a butt but a donkey.) Nannu is teaching me Maltese.

"And besides, you should have heard Sophia."

"Never mind about Sophia," Mom said. "I wanted to remind you to come straight home from school because Nanna and Nannu are coming for supper. Nanna wants to show you and Sophia how to make pastizzi."

A cooking lesson. So that was why Sophia was cranky. She hated cooking, but Nanna thought it was a skill every new bride needed.

"But Biff and I have plans for after school." We needed to brainstorm on how to get Adam to notice me.

Mom said nothing, just looked at me. Guilt. A mother's most powerful weapon.

"Fine." Family before friends, blah, blah, blah, though I have no idea why! I get to pick my friends, while my family got forced onto me. Then I got an idea. "Can Biff come for supper too?" A friend would make family bearable.

"If her mother gives her permission," Mom said.

E-mail
8:00 a.m.
To: Biff
From: T
Subject: Supper

> Ask your mom if you can come to supper tonight. Nanna is making pastizzi. Think of it as an opportunity to examine a tribe of women working together in the kitchen.
> L8R
> T

One advantage of Sophia waking me early is that I got the bathroom before Hugo. He pounded on the door for me to let him in, but I was busy admiring my new womanly curves so I ignored him. I put on lip gloss and blotted it. As I went to throw the tissue into the garbage can, my eye caught a glimpse of plastic beneath an old shampoo bottle. Hugo pounded so hard the door nearly came off the hinges.

"I'll be out in a minute," I yelled.

Now, normally I wouldn't root around in a gross garbage can, but that plastic had me curious. I picked up the shampoo bottle between my thumb and forefinger and saw what looked like a thermometer, but smaller and it had a pink + sign rather than digits.

It took a moment, then OMIGAWD! Not a thermometer—a pregnancy test! I stood up. No way was I touching that. You had to pee on those things to make them work. And then the big OMIDOUBLEGAWD hit me! Someone in this house was having a baby! And it wasn't me. I'm sure I'd remember if I'd had sex. So it had to be—SOPHIA! She and Anthony were having sex, and obviously they hadn't used a *condiment* on his *election*.

Secret: Okay, this is another word I have trouble with: erection. That's the proper name for the male's thingie when it's ready for action. I hear that word, and my cheeks get hot and I giggle like an idiot. So to prevent such embarrassing behavior on my part, I call it an *election*.

I threw the tissue back over the plus sign so Hugo wouldn't see it, then I opened the door and pushed past him. This was huge. I bet even Mom didn't know. Would Sophia fit in her wedding dress? Would I have to wear the puke-green maid of honor dress? Wait until Biff heard.

I grabbed my books, jacket, and lunch and headed out the door. I ran to the corner, only to find I was early so I had to wait for Biff. I was caught up in a tornado of thoughts when I heard a voice behind me.

"Hey, Teresa."

Phillip White! He'd come up while I was distracted by positive-pink-signs-*condiments*-thoughts. I debated stepping around the tree out of his line of vision, but he was standing right beside me and well, that might be a little too obvious.

"Oh. Hi, Phillip," I muttered.

I glanced up and down the street. No one in sight, but I had to get rid of him, fast. I didn't want anyone seeing me talking to a SN. I could be contaminated.

"We're in the same homeroom," Phillip said.

"Are we? I hadn't noticed."

"I guess you're surprised to see me back here."

"Yeah. I guess," I said. *Okay, you're back, now leave!*

He shifted his briefcase to his other hand. I mean, seriously, a briefcase? Why couldn't he have a backpack or book bag like everyone else? Didn't he want to advance to N?

"Mom and I moved back in the summer. Dad left us."

Uncomfortable Moment (UM). What is the proper reply for someone telling you their family is all busted up?

"Oh. Sorry."

Phillip shrugged. "It happens. But hey, here I am back in the old neighborhood."

I smiled weakly.

"You're looking pretty groovy," Phillip said.

GROOVY?? Omigawd! He was staring at my chest. Second UM. I mean, I'd known Phillip so long it was like having my brother suddenly notice I was a girl! Yuck.

Double Omigawd! Ash*la-a-y* was coming up the street! At the center of a pack of ANs that included Hugo and AAA!

I circled behind the trunk out of view of the ANs and pretended to search the treetop.

"What are you doing?" Phillip asked.

"I thought I saw a scarlet tangerine up here," I said.

"That's not a fruit tree," Phillip said.

"The scarlet tangerine *bird*." How could he be so dumb?

I pressed myself against the trunk and peeked out. The ANs were almost level with us. I crept around the trunk, keeping out of view.

"Yeah, well…see you at school, I guess." He shuffled away.

I peered out again. Ashleigh's golden hair swung with every step. She has to have highlights to get that shine. I wonder if Mom would pay for me to get highlights. Or is that a luxury that I needed to get myself? Well, if I was paying for it myself, I was going all blonde.

As I pondered hair color, a body pushed in next to me.

"Are we spying?" Biff asked.

"No, I was just looking for a scarlet tangerine," I explained.

"This area is too far north to grow citrus fruit," Biff said kindly.

"It's a bird!" Didn't people know their birds?

"Do you mean a scarlet tanager?" She glanced at the tree branch. "T, that's a cardinal."

A cardinal? Because Dad hated nature, it was Nannu who took me to the park when I was little and taught me all about birds and, well, nature stuff. And there was that embarrassing Red-Bellied Brown Bird episode in kindergarten when I vehemently disputed the name "robin." Only to find out the teacher was right. When I told Nannu, he said birds had different names in Malta.

Mom told me to not believe everything Nannu said, because he loved to tell tall tales.

"You mean he lies?" I asked her once.

"Not exactly," Mom said. "More like he embellishes. He exaggerates."

I must have looked puzzled.

"Okay. Yes, he lies. But he doesn't mean to. He wants to tell you an exciting story. Though lying is never a good thing," she added hastily.

But there were some things I knew Nannu had not lied about. Like his stories of being a kid and hiding in limestone caves in Malta during World War II while bombs dropped on the island. Or of eating grass because there was no food because of the war, or his mother crying and rocking his baby sister, who died of starvation during the war. Those weren't lies or even exaggerations. I could tell because of the tears in his eyes when he told those stories to me. But Nannu never dwelled on bad memories for long. He'd clap his hands together and say, "But why we sad? Life, it too short. Let's dance." And he'd sweep me up into his arms and waltz me around.

"You're late." I grabbed Biff's arm and hurried her along. I thrust out my chest and led the way with my breasts. She didn't even notice!

"Who was that boy?" Biff asked. "I thought he was talking to a tree until I saw you hiding behind it."

"No one. His name's Phillip. He used to live around here years ago."

"Really? Was there any interaction between him and the group of ANs across the street?" She twisted her backpack around and grabbed a pen and paper.

"Would you stop being an anthropologist for one minute and hurry up?" I snarled. "We'll be late for school."

Biff raised her eyebrows. "Bitchy. PMS-ing?"

There were times I wanted to biff Biff! I stuck my chest out so far I nearly got curvature of the spine.

"Hey."

Finally.

"What did you do?" she squealed, and stared right at my chest. Now, normally Biff and I don't stare at each other's chests, but today I was proud she was looking.

"I grew overnight."

"Yeah, right."

"Okay, last night Sophia and I went to Prim and Proper in the mall and she bought me a new bra. It has air pouches."

"To push up the breasts," Biff said. "That's very innovative. But what if someone sticks a pin in one of them?"

"I guess I'll take off like a pricked balloon!" I yelled. "No one's going to stick a pin in me *there*." Why couldn't she just be happy for me? Or better still, a little bit jealous.

"Well, they look fabulous," Biff declared, and I wasn't mad at her anymore.

"By the way," she went on. "Did I tell you Adam is in my biology class?"

"No!" I shrieked. "Why didn't you say something yesterday? Tell me everything. Omigawd! Does he sit next to any of those stupid eleventh grade AN girls? Do you sit next to him? Does he seem deep and thoughtful? And do I sound desperate?"

"Okay, let me answer those questions in sequential order, since you like lists so much. Number one: I was distracted by our school-supply shopping trip. Number two and three combined: A boy on one side, me on the other."

That is so unfair. Biff getting to sit next to my AAA.

"Number four: I don't know, as we were only in class for ten minutes. Number five: Yes."

She held up her hand to stop me speaking. "I solemnly promise to take copious notes detailing Adam's every move and every word he speaks. How's that? Oh, and his locker is eight down from yours. I hung around after class to see where it was because I knew you'd be interested."

I threw my arms around her neck and nearly strangled her. You can see why I love Biff, in a totally non-lesbian way. We'll be dating in no time. (I mean me and Adam, not me and Biff.)

Unfortunately, I was so excited by the AAA news that I forgot to tell Biff about the whole plus-sign, pregnancy-thermometer-test thing.

6

f is For Family
(you don't get to choose them)

Cheese Pastizzi

2 lbs. flaky pastry dough

(You can buy flaky dough to save time, but don't let Nanna know!)

2 lbs. ricotta cheese

(There is low-fat cheese, Nanna!)

sprinkle of salt

2 eggs

Thoroughly mix ricotta cheese and eggs and add a sprinkle of salt. Roll out the dough (not too thin) and cut in four-inch circles. Put one tablespoon of the ricotta mixture in the middle of each circle. Fold circles over to make a pocket and squeeze edges together to seal. Place on a greased baking sheet and bake at 375°F for approximately an hour. Keep an eye on them, though, as sometimes they are done earlier. Done means golden-brown.

Tip: Eat while warm—yum, lip-smacking good.

"You can't let the dough get dry," Nanna P said. She set a wet tea towel over thin, cream-colored sheets of pastry and pulled a bowl over to her. "Now we mix the filling. Sophia, you do this."

Mom, Grandma T, and I sat at the table, watching Nanna instruct a reluctant Sophia. Biff was there, too, scribbling away furiously in her notebook. Everyone thought she was copying down the recipe. I knew better: anthropologist at work studying the strange tribal customs of women in the kitchen.

Grandma T was there as a result of Mom's delusion.

Mom's Delusion: We are all one big happy family.
Reality: Grandma T's nose gets a better workout than a rabbit's when she's around Nannu, as she sniffs her disapproval of his barbarian manners.

Dad, Hugo, and Nannu were watching TV in the living room.

Sophia grimaced and picked up a spoon. "Anthony doesn't even like pastizzi."

"He's a good Maltese boy. He likes pastizzi," Nanna announced.

"And you know you can buy ready-made pastizzi at the market," Sophia went on.

"Buy it?" Nanna looked horrified. She dumped ricotta cheese into the bowl and cracked two eggs on the side and let the yellow yolks slide in. "It no good if you buy it."

"Actually, it's not bad ... " Sophia began.

"It no good," Nanna declared firmly. "You to be a *gharusa* soon. All brides must know how to make pastizzi for their *gharus*. Husbands expect it. You feed their stomachs. That makes you a good wife. I make it all the time for Pa. Now you mix."

I was glad to be in my kitchen, listening to Nanna scold Sophia, watching Grandma T's nose twitch, and hearing Biff's pen scratch on paper. I needed the distraction. Health class this afternoon had been very embarrassing.

Physical Education: Boys and girls have separate classes.
Health Class (a.k.a. sex education): Boys and girls are together.
Question: What is the school thinking?

So today, in co-ed health class, we had to put *condiments* on bananas. I'm a girl and it felt weird to me, so it must have been doubly weird for the boys. Being compared to a banana, I mean. I opened the flat little package, and slid out the latex—um—*condiment*.

What I Learned in Health Class: When putting a condiment on a banana, do not peel the banana first.

How was I supposed to know you didn't peel the banana? I'd never done this before. Anyway, it broke in half. The banana, not the *condiment*. And I said, "Oh no, it's broken." Everyone laughed and kept repeating, *Oh no, it's broken.* And why bananas? Sex is forever ruined for me. My first time, all I'll think about is fruit. I haven't told Mom yet, but I'm dropping health class. I can't possibly go back there again.

Sophia rolled her eyes and stabbed the spoon into the bowl. "What are you staring at?" she growled at me. "Every time I turn around, you're staring at me."

Psychology 101: Transference. Deflect your anger to younger siblings.

"I'm not staring."

But I was, at her stomach. I was looking for a sign that she was expecting. I was also wondering when she was going to drop the bomb on Mom and Dad. I needed to prod her a bit.

"It's a good thing you're learning to cook. You'll soon be eating for two."

Mom shot me a startled glance.

"What are you babbling about?" Sophia said.

"No. No. Use your hands. They mix best." Nanna thrust Sophia's hands into the slippery mess of egg yolk and cheese.

"Why can't Teresa do it?" Sophia asked.

"Rash." I pointed to my hands. They'd been itchy at supper and now were covered with red spots. "Unhygienic."

Sophia grimaced as she mixed the gloppy mess with her hands, and Biff and I giggled.

Suddenly Mom leaped from her chair and rushed upstairs.

"Is Mom okay?" I asked.

"She fine." Nanna calmly layered pastry and cheese in a casserole dish.

"But her face went all weird," I began.

"She fine," Nanna repeated.

I let it go. If Nanna thought Mom was okay, she had to be. I mean, Mom was her daughter, and Mom always knows when I'm not fine.

Nanna generously dotted butter on top of the pastry. Now it was me grimacing. The fat in the butter and cheese would go directly to my genetically doomed butt. I eyed Nanna's sizable bottom as she bent to put the baking sheet in the oven. I was on bum crunch number eleven when Mom came back into the room. She looked shaky, and a bit green.

"What are you doing?" Sophia asked me.

"Huh?" I said.

"You're going up and down on that chair."

Remember? Transference.

"Bum crunches. Keeping it firm."

"*Stupidu*," Sophia said.

That's a Maltese word that needs no translation.

"Sophia. That's enough," Mom warned. Then, "Teresa, you know you are a beautiful girl. Your bottom is just fine.

We love you the way you are and you should love yourself, too, inside and out."

"Mom, I'm not turning anorexic or anything. I was just exercising." No need to see *someone*.

At that moment Nannu came in and grabbed Nanna's thick waist and spun her around, waltzing in the small space between the table and stove. Nanna and Nannu are both short with round, wrinkled faces and stocky bodies. It was like watching two garden gnomes grapple with each other. Nanna slapped at Nannu's hands, but Nannu just laughed and continued to twirl her around in circles. Biff wrote frantically, no doubt about tribal dances, while the rest of us watched, fascinated, as Nanna and Nannu bumped into the table, upset a bowl, and sent a chair skidding across the floor.

"Pa!" Nanna and Mom cried in unison.

Grandma T's nose just about fell off it twitched so much.

I decided to take advantage of the confusion to do a little propelling of my own, and I swept Biff off her chair and into my bedroom. Time for my version of anthropology. The age-old custom of snaring the male.

During History class, I had drawn up a list of trapping possibilities.

How to be Irresistible to AAA

Plan A: Dye my hair blonde. It's my observation that blondes get the guys more than dark-haired girls. But shouldn't personality count for something? (I threw that last line in for a laugh. I mean, seriously, these are guys we're talking about.)

Plan B: Write a book and become a famous teen author.

Plan C: Play hard to get.

Plan D: Pass his locker every day until he notices me.

Plan E: Get my belly button pierced. (Show my dark side.)

Plan F: Swoon at his feet (like Scarlett O'Hara).

Biff looked through my plans. She immediately dismissed *A*.

"You have beautiful hair," she said. "Leave it alone."

"But blondes always get the guys," I protested.

"So you would change yourself just to get a guy?" Biff asked.

What I thought: Yes, absolutely, if it meant Adam would look at me!

What I said: "I guess not."

She read Plan B. "You're going to write a book?"

"I could write a book," I protested, hurt that she had so little faith in me. "How hard can it be?"

"What would you write about?"

"Well, I'd write about..." Hmm...good question. I hadn't given much thought as to what I would write. I was more caught up in the after-writing drama of interviews on late night talk shows, or early morning talk shows, signing copies of my book for my fans, Mom and Dad tearful with pride.

"It takes at least a year if not longer to write a book," Biff said. "And that's if you already have a theme or subject in mind."

"A picture book, then. They're small."

"No book." She was firm about that.

Plan C—"He doesn't know you're alive, so how can you be hard to get?"

Plan D—"He'll think you're a stalker."

Plan E—"You're scared of needles. You don't even have pierced ears! Besides, we can't show navels at school." I had forgotten about the *stupidu* Dress Code.

Plan F—"When you swoon, you'll bang your head on the floor and knock yourself out. He'll trip over you."

She had been crossing out the plans with heavy black marker as she discarded each one. By the end I was left with, well, exactly nothing!

"I do have a Plan G," she said.

Good ol' Biff.

Plan G: OPERATION AAAA (Attract Achingly Adorable Adam)

The name of the plan was my idea. A secret code in case we needed to confer at school and not have everyone know what we were talking about. Biff complained that it sounded like we were seriously, seriously recovering alcoholics. Too bad. I'm sticking with it.

Objective: To make Adam aware of my existence.

Method: Biff would accidentally-on-purpose leave her Biology book with me. I'd have to come to her class to return it to her. I would be wearing my new jeans, and black boots to give me height.

Mental Note to Self: Buy black boots.
Second Mental Note to Self: Need money for black boots. Babysit D and D.

Also, the cute top that I'd lost, but found when I was looking for Ken.

I would go to Biff's Biology class and she would come up and take the book and say, "Thank you very much, Teresa," in a loud voice so Adam would know my name. I also wanted her to say, "You're such a wonderful friend," but she thought that was overkill.

"Wouldn't it be cool," I said, "if right now, Adam was working on an operation to make me aware of his existence. Maybe he'd call it TTTT. Trapping Totally Terrific Teresa."

"I don't think boys do that," Biff said. "They wouldn't bother to go to so much trouble."

"So, it's only girls that do this stuff?" I asked.

"That's what my findings are telling me," she said.

"Why?"

"I'm not sure yet. Further research is required, but I believe it has to do with self-esteem issues."

Oh yeah. Self-esteem. I knew all about that from Mom. Boring.

"We should practice what I'm going to say to Adam if he talks to me," I said. I grabbed my Barbie and Ken dolls off the shelf and handed Ken to Biff. "You be Adam."

Biff swung Ken around by his leg. "Aren't we a little old for playing dolls?"

"We're not playing dolls. We're role-playing. Psychologists use it as a technique all the time, and they're adults."

"Psychologists have Barbie and Ken dolls in their offices?" Biff said.

"Just role-play."

Biff can be so annoying at times.

I danced Barbie across the bed and flung the doll's blonde hair. "I'm Ash*la-a-y.*"

Biff giggled.

"Okay, seriously now," I said. "Pretend this is the school hall and the doll is me, and I'm walking by Adam's locker."

"Hi there, Teresa." Biff lowered her voice an octave.

"Oh, sorry, do I know you?" I asked. I turned Barbie toward Ken.

"Well, you should. You think about me constantly and walk past my locker a hundred times a day," Biff/Ken said.

I whacked Ken with my Barbie.

"Oh, you're hot, TTT," Biff/Ken said.

"I am hot. Who turned up the heat in here?" I/Barbie said in a sexy voice.

I pulled off the doll's sweater and threw it at Ken.

"Give me some more of that," Biff/Ken said.

Barbie strutted across the bed, taking off her clothing and tossing it at Ken.

"I'm Stripper Barbie," I yelled.

Biff was on the floor laughing when suddenly she stopped, and her eyes widened as she looked over my shoulder.

I turned, and there was Mom in the doorway.

"Oh, hi," I said. "Biff and I were just playing ... dolls," I finished lamely.

Mom's eyebrows disappeared under her bangs. I could see the speculation in her eyes: *someone.* "Biff, your father's here to take you home."

Red-faced, Biff grabbed her backpack, stowed her pencil and notebook inside, then smacked the Velcro fastening in place.

We followed Mom downstairs to find Biff's father at the door. Dad stood at the bottom of the steps, swaying back and forth, hands fidgeting, eyes frantically combing the room, desperate to find something—anything—to say to Biff's father. Social phobia, remember? Except Dad says it's not a phobia, he just can't think of anything to say to people he's not really that interested in and probably will never see again, so why make the effort? How lame does that sound? In this case, I think Mom's diagnosis is right.

Nanna rushed up with a package for Biff. Nannu followed in hot pursuit. "Come dance with me, *sabih.*"

"That means 'beautiful' in Maltese," I whispered to Biff.

"Pa, stop it," Nanna said. She thrust the bundle at Biff. "Some pastizzi for you and your family."

Nannu wrapped his arm around Nanna and twirled her away, knocking books off the coffee table as they passed. Biff's father stared in amazement. Obviously, he'd never seen garden gnomes dance.

Sweat ran down Dad's face as he struggled to get a few words out. Mom nodded encouragingly at him. Grandma T looked dazed. I've come to the conclusion she thinks we're from another planet, and we abducted her son and changed him to be like us. Evil aliens.

Biff pushed her father toward the door. "Thanks for supper, Mrs. Tolliver. See you tomorrow, T."

Dad's mouth finally moved and he shouted out the door after them, "So, what's with those snakes, eh?"

"Snakes?" I heard Biff's father say as they went down the porch steps. "What's he talking about? Snakes?"

"Honestly," Mom said as she closed the door. "Pa, dancing all over the place, and you, Marshall..." She shook her head in disgust. "Snakes! You insulted his religion."

I felt really bad and almost told Mom not to worry about it, because Biff's dad was an atheist and had no religion, but I bit my tongue in time.

It wasn't until later, when I was in bed, that I realized Sophia never had admitted that she was pregnant, and I had once again forgotten to tell Biff!

g is For gROSS

It took me three weeks to work up the nerve to put Operation AAAA into, well, operation. Every day Biff would say, "What about today?" and I'd find an excuse why that particular day was no good.

First Excuse: I had to get over the trauma of wearing my air-bra. It took me almost two weeks to get used to having breasts. Every time I looked down, I'd get a shock.
Second Excuse: The thongs. It took another week to get rid of that permanent wedgie feeling. Major stress!

But when I met Biff at the corner this morning, instead of "What about today?" she said, "Today is the day."

Sweat trickled from my armpits right down to my waist.

By some weird stroke of fate, gym class became a study hall because Miss Cook had to go for professional help. She called it professional *development,* but we all know it's *help.*

I stood by my locker as the hall emptied out. My heart thudded so hard my chest ached. I could barely breathe. I usually reserve this amount of anxiety for big stuff, like telling a lie (or the truth) or taking an exam, but Operation AAAA was the hugest thing I'd ever done. I clung to my locker door as a wave of giddiness swept over me.

"You okay? You look sort of odd." Phillip slammed shut his locker and leaned against it. Another stroke of fate —ill this time. Phillip's locker was two down from mine. Why couldn't it be Adam's locker?

"Fine. I'm fine."

"No gym today?" he asked.

I shook my head. "No. We have study hall instead." I wished he'd go away. I needed to be alone to have a nervous breakdown.

"Well," I said, "I guess I'll go to study hall now." *Hint. Hint.* But Phillip never moved. "Oh, I have to take a book to Biff first. She accidentally left her Biology text with me ... accidentally."

"I'm heading to Math. It's right next to the Biology lab. I can give it to her," Phillip offered.

"That's okay," I said. "I'll do it."

"Really. It's no problem at all. Save you the trip." He

looked as eager as a puppy wanting to please its master. Pathetic!

"I have to ask her for something, too," I said.

"I can do that for you," Phillip said.

A puppy with a bone. I'd have to revert to something drastic.

"Okay. Ask her if she has any spare tampons," I said.

Phillip's face blanched. I had hit on the perfect solution. No guy in his right mind would walk into a Biology lab and ask a girl if she had a tampon.

"Yeah. Well. Okay. You might want to do that yourself." He turned and fled down the hall.

Alone once again, I dug out the list I'd prepared.

Operation AAAA Checklist

1. Biology book. Check.
2. Hair looking fabuloso. It should be, after an hour in the bathroom with a straightener, Hugo pounding on the door. Check.
3. Breath fresh. I popped a mint. Check.
4. Pants zipper done up. Check and double check. (If you ever have a list with this on it, check it twice. Very important.)
5. Bright smile and intelligent look in eyes. Always. Check.

I was ready for the Important First Meeting (IFM).

I sauntered down the corridor and up the stairs to the Biology lab. My hair, shiny and smooth, swung back and forth seductively. Arriving at the door to the classroom, I pushed it open and strode in confidently, my new boots making my legs look long and lean in my jeans, with no VPL (Visible Panty Line) because of the thong. I stood for a moment, trying to find Biff.

Adam came up to me and asked, "Can I help you?" He glanced at my air-enhanced breasts (empowered woman).

"I'm looking for Elizabeth," I said, voice low and sultry.

"She's over by the windows." Adam pointed.

I walked away, throwing a casual, "Thanks" over my shoulder.

"No problem," he said, and watched me cross the classroom, totally entranced.

Later that afternoon he begged Biff to tell him all about me, and we started dating the next day.

Okay, that was the fantasy.

Here's the reality.

I slammed my locker shut and started to strut away, but my arm jerked back and the Biology book flew across the hall. The sleeve of my sweater was caught in the locker door. I freed myself and stooped to pick up the book, which really made the thong dig in.

I scuttled down the corridor and up the stairs. Outside the Biology lab door, I took a deep breath, tried to work the worst of the wedgie out (belatedly remembering the surveillance cameras), and opened the door to the classroom.

Chaos. Desk and chair legs screeched as they scraped over the floor. Loud male voices shouted, and girls' shrill laughs soared over everything. I ducked a paper missile launched at my head and tried to find Biff in the crowd. And then I saw him. Adam.

He was sitting on a desk talking to another boy. Suddenly, he threw his head back and laughed. Omigawd! He was gorgeous. Beautiful—though in a manly way. Instant brain-freeze.

Mr. Sackett, the Biology teacher, walked into the classroom, gave me a curious look, and yelled at the class to quiet down. After everyone had found their seats, he turned to me.

"Yes?"

I stared at him. What *was* I doing there? I heard a snicker.

"Oh, I think Teresa brought my Biology textbook. I forgot it." And Biff was beside me.

I grinned at her stupidly. Yes, of course, her textbook. I hung on to it—my prop—for dear life.

"Thank you, Teresa," Biff said. She tugged at the book, but I cradled it closer to my chest. Suddenly there was a loud pop, a hiss, and I felt my left breast deflate. A sharp end of the metal binding on the book had pierced the air pouch in my bra!

"Hey, I think she blew up," someone said.

I stood there, smiling madly. Biff looked stricken. She knew if she took the book, I'd look lopsided.

"Uh ... never mind," Biff said. "You can have the text-book. I'll get it from you later."

I nodded. The class was laughing out loud now.

"Leave," Biff whispered. She gave me a shove toward the door and I stumbled out.

I slumped against the beige wall, then turned and banged my forehead against it. Idiot. Loser. *Stupidu.* Well, that was it! I'd be an SN for sure now. I stared at my deflated left breast. I couldn't face study hall lopsided.

I gathered up my books and left a Post-it on Biff's locker.

"GONE HOME!"

• • • • •

The house was empty. Real empty. I needed chocolate chip peanut butter cookies. And milk. I needed someone to fuss around me, like when I was sick. I telephoned Mom at the bank.

"Teresa," Mom said. "What's wrong?"

"Nothing's wrong," I snapped. Why did she automatically assume something was wrong?

"I just wanted to tell you that I'm going over to Nanna and Nannu's for a bit." I crossed my fingers. "We got out early because gym was cancelled. Miss Cook's gone to get professional help."

"That's fine, honey. Are you sure you're okay?"

"Of course I'm okay. Honestly, Mom." I'd just embarrassed myself in front of the entire school, had no breasts, and ruined my chances with AAA forever, but I was fine. I hung up, mad at Mom though I knew that didn't make sense. But it was better than being mad at me. Transference.

I didn't have money for bus fare, so I'd have to walk the ten blocks to Nanna and Nannu's apartment. The sky had clouded over and a stiff breeze smelled of damp. October gray sky, bare gray tree branches, cold wind—it all added to my misery. I huddled into my jacket. The first fat drops of rain hit me with five blocks still to go. I didn't run or even walk faster, because I wanted to get wet. If you're going to have a self-pity party, make it a good one. But the deluge held off until after I got to Nanna and Nannu's apartment, and I arrived dry and disgruntled.

As soon as I stepped off the elevator on the twentieth floor, I was enveloped in a heady aroma of tomato and basil. I sniffed deeply, and immediately felt better. Nanna stood at the door to their apartment, wooden spoon in hand. She took my coat and hung it in the closet. I went into the living room.

Through the large picture window I could see the city spread below: cars scurrying down streets like beetles, people running about like ants. I never tired of watching it. When I get a job, I am going to have my own apartment on the twentieth floor. Then I will be able to look down on the world and its people. Oh, when I say *look down,* I mean it literally, not *look down on them* as in *I'm better than them.*

"Teresa, come sit here." Nannu patted the sofa beside

him. "Come watch the weather on television. It going to rain today in Sydney, Australia, but India is going to be hot."

Nannu was a great fan of the Weather Channel.

"She doesn't want to watch your weather," Nanna said.

She steered me ahead of her into the kitchen and pushed me into a chair. She opened the refrigerator and took out a carton of milk. "Fiona called and said you were coming to visit us. What's wrong?"

Honestly, Mom! "Nothing is wrong," I insisted. But it came out loud. Way too loud.

Nanna poured a glass of milk for me and put a tin of home-baked cookies on the table, then went back to stir a pot of tomato sauce on the stove. Nannu turned off the television, and pulled out a chair beside me and dropped into it. He grabbed a cookie from the tin and munched away, leaving crumbs scattered over his shirt front, all the while studying my face.

"Boys," he said finally, with a hint of triumph in his voice. "Is boys, Maria."

Nanna shrugged. "Of course. It's always a boy."

I rolled my eyes.

Nannu's hand hovered over the cookie tin, but Nanna rapped his knuckles with her wooden spoon. "You get fat. Remember what the doctor say."

"Boys, right?" He grinned at me, and I couldn't help but smile back.

"Yes, a boy," I admitted.

"You like him, but he don't like you."

"How did you know that?" I asked.

"I have five girls. All of them look like you at one time. I know."

"Well, it's not that he doesn't like me, he just doesn't know I exist," I said.

"Ah." Nannu leaned back in his chair and sighed. "The greatest loves are those kept in secret. Don't worry. You a beautiful girl. He doesn't know what he missing."

"She too young anyway," Nanna said. She put an arm around my shoulders and squeezed. "You too young to be thinking of boys."

"Hah! You were her age when you make eyes at me," Nannu said.

"I never make eyes at you," Nanna said, outraged. She turned back to the stove and stirred her pot fiercely.

"She make eyes at me," Nannu whispered across the table.

I felt so much better.

"Where the newspaper, Maria?" Nannu asked. "I want to see who died."

Nanna picked up the paper from the counter and slapped it down in front of him.

As soon as Nanna's back was turned, he fished in the tin for a cookie.

"Maria. Where the newspaper?" He said again.

I stared at him. "It's right in front of you."

"Oh, so it is." Nannu licked his finger, then used it to turn pages until he got to the obituaries.

"He forget everything," Nanna said. "Yesterday, he look for car keys and they right in his hand!"

"Ach." Nannu waved a disgusted hand in Nanna's direction, then bent his head and read the first obituary.

"You don't know any of those people," I pointed out to him.

"Doesn't matter," Nannu said. "I like to see who died."

"That's morbid," I said.

"I look at their years. If older than me, then I have a few more years left. If younger, I outlive them. Either way I feel good."

You couldn't argue with that.

• • • • •

Dad picked me up on his way home from work. I came down to meet him with my arms full of containers of tomato sauce and cookies. We made our way through the cookies as he slowly drove the ten blocks home—a three-cookie ride, we discovered.

"We'll ruin our supper," Dad said.

"Yep," I agreed.

While Mom heated up the spaghetti sauce for supper, I went on the computer. Biff was already on.

MSN Message:

Biff said: T!!! WHERE R U????

T said: I was at Nanna and Nannu's apartment. BTW am quitting school.

Biff said: R U SURE???? OPERATION AAAA success-
fully completed.

I blinked and looked at the computer screen. Successful?
Was that a typo?

T said: Repeat.

Biff said: AAA asked me about you.

OMIGAWD! Adam knows I'm alive! Forget the computer.
This called for a real-life, um ... telephone call. I ran for
the stairs.

"Teresa, you could set the table for me," Mom called.

"In a minute, I have to call Biff."

"You can call Biff after supper. I need the table set now."

"Mom, this is an emergency. It's about school," I
added.

Mom came out and steered me by the shoulders into
the kitchen. "Supper first. It's important we get together as
a family at least once a day to connect with each other ... "
And after that pretty much all I heard was "blah, blah,
blah ... "

I stomped around, throwing knives and forks on the
table and banging plates down. Yes, it was a childish tan-
trum, and to give Mom credit, she did a pretty good job
of ignoring me.

I wolfed down my spaghetti, though still noted Nanna's wonderful tomato sauce flavored with basil, oregano,
and garlic (yum), and dashed to the phone before Hugo

could get to it. Closing my bedroom door, I dragged my dresser in front of it so no one could get in. I set Barbie and Ken on my bed and pulled the covers over our heads.

I was now ready for: THE MOST IMPORTANT TELEPHONE CALL OF MY LIFE.

Me: Okay, every inglesay etailday.

Biff: How did you know I was going to pick up the phone? It might have been my mom or dad.

Me: Every inglesay etailday!

Biff: If you're going to speak in easily decipherable code, I'm ending this phone call right now.

Me: It's obvious you are an only child. If you had siblings you'd know exactly why I was speaking in *code,* as you call it. That would make a good anthropological study for you: siblings. (I said that last bit a little nastily, though Barbie was grinning—she has a younger sister.)

Biff: Hanging up now.

Me: I'm sorry. I'm sorry. Really, I'm sorry. (Excessive grovelling, I know, but I was in danger of losing my only pipeline of information.)

Biff: Very well.

Me: Every single detail.

Biff: After you left, Adam asked me who you were and I told him you were my friend, Teresa. He said you were quite funny.

Dead silence.

Me: And???

Biff: That's it.

Obviously Biff didn't have a clue what "every single detail" meant. I'd have to draw it out of her.

Me: Let's begin again. What was he wearing?

Biff: You were there. You saw what he was wearing.

Me: Okay. What was I wearing?

Biff: What? You know what you were wearing. You dressed yourself!

Biff was getting tetchy (Grandma T's word).

Me: I was just setting the scene. When he asked who I was, did he sound interested, like "Who was that cool chick?" Or, was it more like, "Who *was* that?" so he could avoid me from now on?

Biff: The former.

I had to think for a moment as to what "the former" meant, and then I excitedly banged Barbie and Ken's lips together in a kiss.

Me: Did he like my jeans? My new boots?

Biff: He didn't say, though he did ask what the popping sound was.

Disaster! I unlatched Barbie's mouth from Ken's.

Biff: I told him it was my textbook binding popping and you kept the book to repair it for me.

Me: Oh, thank you! You saved my life!

Biff: I did, didn't I? Not only did I quickly think up an explanation, but I showed you in a generous light, also. A helping friend.

Barbie and Ken grappled frantically, Ken trying to rip Barbie's top from her perfect breasts.

Breasts! *Oh No!*

Me: My bra is wrecked! What am I going to wear to school tomorrow?

Biff: Only one side is wrecked.

Me: So, I go to school with one perky breast and one flat one?

Barbie stuck out her perfect breasts for me to see, while Biff and I pondered the bra dilemma.

Biff: Maybe you could duct tape the hole and re-inflate it with a bicycle pump…

Me: No.

Silence.

Me: Did you know that Barbie doesn't have any nipples?

Biff: Huh?

Me: Barbie doesn't have any nipples. She's not perfect. And why is the nipple the naughty part? I mean, it's perfectly fine for everyone to see every part of your boob, except the nipple? That little thing is the dirty part.

Biff: It's weird, isn't it? Guys will give anything to see a nipple.

Me: I have a rash all up my arms.

Biff: Maybe you have hives from nerves.

I heard Dad calling for me from downstairs.

Me: I gotta go.

Biff: Stuff a sock in it.

Me: What?

I thought she was being rude.

Biff: Stuff a sock in your bra!

I was rolling around on the bed laughing when Dad pushed at the door. It hit the dresser with a bang.

"What is this here for?" he asked, through a crack.

"Early-warning signal," I told him. "People are always bursting into my room with no respect for my privacy."

"Family meeting. Downstairs. Now. And put your furniture back in place."

Me: See you tomorrow, Biff.

I hung up the phone and dragged my dresser away from the door, and followed Dad to the kitchen.

Sophia and Mom sat at the table, Sophia dressed to go out, fingers tapping impatiently, wanting to be with her precious Anthony. He probably wouldn't mind that she was late if it delayed a painfully slow death-by-wedding-details.

Hugo rooted in the fridge. (How could he be hungry? We just had supper!) "Hockey practice tonight, Dad. I have to be there in half an hour."

"And I have a date with Anthony," Sophia said. "I'm a little old for family meetings."

"This will only take a minute," Mom told her. "And you're never too old for family. We're always here for each other."

I plopped in a chair and studied Sophia and Hugo. Neither looked guilty, though Sophia looked a little wary. I knew what she was thinking: this was all about her wedding.

Honestly, she was so self-absorbed. It was obviously all about me. But what had I done?

"This will only take a minute," Mom said. "Your father and I have some news."

OMIGAWD! The pregnancy test! In all the excitement of AAA liking me and my deflated bra, I'd almost forgotten. I sat back, preparing to enjoy myself.

"Don't you mean *Sophia* has some news?" I said.

Mom looked puzzled. "No. Your father and I. Good news."

"What?" I exclaimed. "I put a dresser in front of my door for privacy and Dad yells at me, but Sophia is having extramarital sex and a BABY and you think that's good news?"

"It is premarital sex, you idiot," Sophia spat out.

Mom's mouth fell open.

"Not that Anthony and I are doing that," Sophia hastily added. "Well, there isn't any baby."

"I saw the pregnancy test in the bathroom. And it was *positive.*" Let's see her get out of that one.

"It wasn't mine," Sophia said.

"Well, it certainly wasn't mine. And there's only two females in this house," I finished grandly.

"Three," Mom said.

It took us a minute, but we eventually put it together.

Sophia looked horrified. Dad had a silly grin on his face, and Hugo was anxious to get to hockey.

"You're going to have a baby?" Sophia yelled.

Mom nodded. "In the spring."

"That is absolutely disgusting," Sophia went on. "You're ... you're both ... old!" She turned on Dad. "I thought you would have had that fixed by now!"

"Fixed? Why fix what's obviously not broke."

"So the parental units made a little boo-boo," Hugo said. "No big deal. Now let's go, Dad, or I'll miss hockey."

"A baby. In the spring," Sophia went on.

"In March," Mom said. "Or ... "

"What!" Sophia shrieked.

"This is a big change for us as a family," Mom went on. "Dad and I were just as surprised as you are, as we didn't exactly plan for another baby. I thought I had a stomach bug, so it took me a while to figure it out and get used to the idea. But, as I said, this is a big change, so if anyone wants to see *someone* to sort out their feelings—"

"I'm good with it," Hugo said. "Dad—hockey. Can I drive?" Now that he had his learner's permit, Hugo wanted to drive everywhere. Cars and hockey. That's all he cared about.

"You'll be eight months pregnant at my wedding!" Sophia was still shrieking. "My mother, eight months pregnant at my wedding! It's gross! Truly gross. I'll be a laughing stock. I'll have to cancel the wedding. How could you do this to me?"

"Dad!" Hugo picked up his equipment bag from the floor and moved toward the door. The drama was over for him. It was left to the women to get hysterical now.

"You are so selfish, the both of you," I said. "Sophia and her wedding, and Hugo and his hockey. That's all you think about. What about me?" I threw my arms out dramatically. "I've been the baby of this family for nearly fifteen years and suddenly I'm to be a middle child because of a boo-boo. That's the kind of trauma people see *someone* for years to overcome. And I'll probably have to babysit for the rest of my teen years. There goes my social life."

Mom stood up, tears streaming down her face, and fled the kitchen. We heard her footsteps on the stairs.

Dad's face clouded over, a huge storm approaching. Dad didn't get mad often, but when he did—watch out! We all drew back and huddled together.

"I can't believe you kids. You've upset your mother. She's already not feeling well and you just made her feel worse."

You know that expression, "You could hear a pin drop"? Well, that applied right now.

"Sophia, Teresa. Clear the table and clean up those dishes."

"I have hockey practice, Dad," Hugo said, quite subdued for him.

"Yes. So you've told me a dozen times. I'm disappointed with all of you." Dad shook his head and left, Hugo trailing behind.

Dad being disappointed was worse than Dad being mad at me.

Sophia began to stack plates. I rinsed them and put them in the dishwasher.

"A baby might be sort of fun," I said.

Sophia glared at me.

"Is it dangerous for Mom to have a baby at her age?" I asked.

Mom was forty-two.

Sophia stopped gathering forks and knives. After a moment she said, "Mom will be fine. She's healthy."

I opened the fridge and got out the jar of dill pickles. I fished out the biggest one and wrapped it in paper toweling to stop the pickle-juice drips.

"What are you doing?" Sophia asked.

"Pregnant women like pickles."

I carried it upstairs to Mom and Dad's room. Mom lay on the bed, staring at the ceiling. Now that I knew about the baby, I could see the small bump of her stomach. I lay down beside her.

"I brought you a pickle," I said. "Pregnant women like pickles. Right? And I'm sorry for being selfish. I'll help out whenever you want and even babysit, if I don't have a date. Dates come first, okay?" I took a bite of the pickle. Then a second one.

Mom laughed softly and wrapped an arm around me and pulled me tight into her side. "It's a bit scary, isn't it?"

"Even for you?" I asked.

"Yes, even for me."

I felt the bed rock and raised my head to see Sophia

sitting on the opposite edge, pickle in her hand. "I brought you a pickle too, and I'm sorry, Mom. I'm just so stressed about this wedding. I want everything to be perfect." Sophia took a bite out of her pickle.

"I want everything to be perfect for you too, honey," Mom said. "But more importantly, I want you to be happy. Perfect is a pretty high bar to set."

Mom pulled Sophia down beside her and the three of us lay together.

"Well, I know who will be happy," I said. "Father Bernie."

"Yeah, well, maybe Father Bernie should try pushing a baby out of his..." Sophia stopped when Mom turned a look on her.

"So, what are we going to have?" Sophia asked. "A girl or a boy?"

"A girl," I answered quickly. "Who wants another Hugo?"

"My girls." Mom laughed and hugged us.

And the three of us lay there, Mom with a new baby growing inside her, and Sophia and I munching on pickles.

h is For HOrrORSCOPe

You are in for a bumpy ride today. You are apt to be rather irritable and edgy and at odds with others. You can't seem to ignore problems or just let them pass. Relations are tense.

Why do I read my horoscope? If it's bad, I spend the day expecting the sky to fall. And if it's good, I spend the day with very high expectations, only to have them dashed, thus the sky still falls. But every morning before school I read my horoscope. Mom says the predictions are purposely ambiguous so that they can apply to anyone and any situation, so we shouldn't believe them, but I see her sneaking a peek at *her* horoscope before she goes to work. I'm waiting for the horoscope that says: *Today the man of your dreams will tell you he loves you. By the way, that man's name is ADAM.*

I was bursting to tell Biff about the baby. I never did get a chance to tell her about the pregnancy test, but this was way better anyhow.

Excited, I ran out the front door. Mrs. Middleton was chasing an underwear-clad twin around the front lawn with his school clothes in her hand.

"Hi Teresa," she called. "Don't forget you're babysitting this evening. You haven't forgotten, have you?" She sounded desperate.

"I'll be there at seven," I yelled back. I was desperate too—for money. Maybe I could tie the twins to chairs for the evening.

Biff was waiting at the corner—but so was Phillip. *Like he had been for the past three weeks.* Overnight it seemed our twosome had become a threesome. And worse, despite my subtle hints—like, "Get lost, Phillip,"—he showed no signs of leaving.

When I complained to Biff about Phillip (when he wasn't around; I'm not totally insensitive), she shrugged and said, "So he walks to school with us. Big deal. Besides, it's your fault."

"What?"

"Surely you knew? He has a thing for you. That's why he's always hanging around. He feels about you like you do about Adam."

First reaction: EEEWWWWW!

Second reaction: EEEWWWWW!

I was so disgruntled, and more than a little uncomfortable, that I actually sulked all the way to school. And it was a great sulk. I walked a couple of steps behind Biff and Phillip, dragging my feet and obviously ignoring them—but sighing loudly enough to let them know I was there. At one point, Phillip turned around and asked if I wanted him to carry my backpack since I was so tired. I glared at him, and he said, "Guess not." By now anyone else would have figured out that he wasn't welcome, but Phillip was so *stupidu*.

I kept that wonderful sulk up until we got to within a block of school. Then I ran to catch up to them. It would never do to arrive at school alone.

I felt out of sorts all day—edgy and irritable, exactly like my horoscope said. I did a walk-by Adam's locker and he was there, so I flashed him a HUGE smile. He didn't even notice me. I guess I expected more, though I don't know why. After all, he doesn't know that he's my almost-boyfriend. Okay, that sounded creepy, and sort of stalker-ish, but you know what I mean.

Finally, it was the last class of the day and I sat on the gym floor listening to Miss Cook explain the rules for dodge ball. Well, what I was really doing was wallowing in a huge self-pity party for one. It's not like I was missing anything. What kind of rules do you need for dodge ball? If the ball comes at you, get out of the way. If you have the ball, throw it at someone. What's so hard about that?

Suddenly, Ashleigh leaned toward me and said, "Who knew they had rules for dodge ball?"

I looked all around me to see who she was talking to, then turned back to find her smiling right at me. At *me*.

"Yeah, who knew," I croaked.

Now, you have to understand: Ashleigh Harcourt has never spoken to me in my entire high school life of one year. I mean, she's an AN and I'm an N. I went quickly from shock to suspicion. Was it a setup? Was I being singled out to get pulverized at dodge ball? I bent over and discreetly checked that the sock stuffed in my bra was secure.

Rules explained, Miss Cook named Ashleigh (naturally) and another girl, Natalie, as captains of two teams. In our gym class was a rather large-boned (polite) or fat (impolite) girl called Big Bertha, so I knew I would not be the last to be picked for a team, but I was totally knocked for a loop when Ashleigh picked me fourth, after the Glams. I needed Biff's expertise. Only an anthropologist could make sense of this anomaly in the high school class system. I crept over to Ashleigh's team. This was going to be bad.

As usual, Big Bertha was the last woman standing, and by default, ended up on our team.

"Balls must hit the floor before the person," Miss Cook ordered. "No direct throws and no hits to the head." She blew hard on her whistle and I braced for the first slam of the ball. Instead, I felt my arm grabbed and I was shoved behind Big Bertha.

"Stay here with us and you won't get hit," Dumb Glam Melanie whispered. We all crowded behind Big Bertha. She was an easy target to hit, big and slow moving.

After Big Bertha got hit a few times, I said, "Isn't she supposed to get out of the circle once she's hit?"

"Nope. She stays right here as our shield," Melanie said. "We changed the rules. The other team doesn't care because it means they always win. We don't mind losing just as long as our noses don't get hit!"

"What about Miss Cook?" I asked. "Doesn't she notice?"

Melanie shrugged.

I giggled with the others as Big Bertha took a hit in the stomach that pushed her breath out with a *whoosh*, yet at the same time I wondered what it would be like to be inside that body, waddling, made fun of, craving food. I knew where that came from: my conscience.

A Conscience: It helps you resist temptation, stand firm, know right from wrong, say NO to boys (just once I'd like a boyfriend to say no to), and say no to drugs and alcohol.

That's a lot of NOs. But the truth is, my conscience has never done me any great favors in the past. It's mostly made me feel annoyed and miserable, so I wasn't about to let it push me out of the shelter of Big Bertha just to get slammed by a ball.

"Switch sides," Miss Cook yelled. "You need to move, girls, if you don't want to get hit. That's the entire point of the game—to get you moving."

It struck me as odd that she hadn't told my team to move when we were all huddled behind Bertha. Was Miss Cook scared of Ashleigh? I studied the gym teacher. Thin to the point of scrawny, hair wispy and dyed crayon red, she tried to fit in with the kids by dressing in T-shirts and TTPs (Too Tight Pants). She'd probably been an N in her school days, desperately wanting to be an AN. Weird to think of a grown-up being desperate. I mean, she's *grown up!*

Miss Cook blew her whistle.

I grabbed a ball, and was getting ready to hurl it when I saw Big Bertha just standing there. Excess weight kept her from bending to get a ball from the floor. My conscience nudged me, then whacked me hard across the back of my head when I didn't take notice the first time. I tossed Big Bertha my ball. She caught it, looked at me, then threw it back.

She said: "It's just a dumb game."
What she meant: "I don't need your charity."

And that really pissed me off. Big Bertha wasn't supposed to reject ME. She was supposed to be grateful for any scraps of goodwill I sent her way. I hurtled the ball as hard as I could at a girl on the other team and caught her full in the face. She grabbed her nose and bent over, crying. Another girl put an arm around the injured girl's shoulders, then glared at me.

Miss Cook's whistle pierced the gym. "Hey! Bounce those balls first, girls. Whoever threw that ball, you're out of the game. Go sit down."

I gulped back tears. I didn't know why I'd thrown the ball that hard. I didn't even know the girl I'd hit. It was— mean.

"Good hit," Ashleigh called.

I smiled weakly and sat on a bench at the side of the gym.

In the locker room I dressed slowly, fiddling with the zipper of my jeans, wasting time. I hoped Phillip would get tired of waiting for me and walk home on his own. I really needed to talk to Biff. As my best friend, she would wait for me no matter how long I took.

"See you Monday, Teresa," Ashleigh called on her way out.

I really, REALLY needed to talk to Biff. About everything. And I hadn't even told her about the baby yet. I grabbed my pack and swung it over my shoulder and pushed open the locker room doors. There was Biff—and Phillip. They were grinning and laughing at something on a piece of paper in Phillip's hand.

"Hey, T," Phillip called. He waved the paper. "You got to see this! Biff thinks it's hilarious."

Biff?

"Why are you calling her Biff?" I shouted. I marched over to him. "She's my best friend. Not yours. I get to call her Biff, not you. And you don't get to call me 'T,' either. That's Biff's name for me."

Shocked, they both stared at me.

"Oh, never mind," I said. "I'm going home."

I stepped backwards and collided with a body. The impact sent me flying across the hall, to land painfully on my butt next to a vending machine. Dazed, I sat a moment. A hand reached out and grabbed my arm and hauled me up.

"Hey Greg, man, watch where you're going!" a male voice shouted.

I looked up. O-MI-GAWD! It was AAA.

"You okay?" he asked.

I opened my mouth, but nothing would come out. Nothing!

He picked up my backpack (yes, he touched MY backpack) and handed it to me.

"Sorry about that," he said. "Greg's an idiot."

I found my voice. "Thanks," I said.

Wait, that's what I meant to say.

What I really said: "Ta."

In my Grandma T's voice. I was talking England-English. I have no idea where that came from. Maybe I'd bumped my head (yes, I know I fell on my butt, but it was a hard impact!) and it jiggled my brain, and brought out Dad's English side.

Adam grinned at me. "Yeah, ta," he repeated. "Teresa. Right?" OMIDOUBLEGAWD! He knew my name. "Cute."

Farther down the hall, Greg snatched Phillip's briefcase and slammed it against a wall. It burst apart and books and paper flew everywhere. "Hey, Maggot!" he shouted. "You dropped your stuff." A page floated toward me and landed at my feet.

"See you around." Adam caught up with his friends and left, and the hall was quiet.

Like a good SN, Phillip said nothing. He scrambled on all fours on the floor, collecting pages. Biff helped him. I crouched and picked up the sheet at my feet, and slowly walked over to Phillip.

"Total jerks," Biff said, holding a fistful of papers out to him.

Phillip's face was set in stone, eyes dead-flat, resigned. Maggot. That's what they used to call him in fifth grade. You'd think after five years people would have forgotten.

Biff studied him with concern. "Phillip. Ignore them. They're morons. Right, T?"

I hesitated, and saw the surprise in Biff's eyes and the hurt in Phillip's. I handed him the paper.

"Uh, right," I said. "Morons."

9

i is For Introspection AnD iDiot

Sunday afternoon, and Hugo and I were sitting in the back seat of the car on the way to Aunt Grace's. Like we had every single Sunday of my life. First church, then off to Aunt Grace's for a family dinner. It's pretty sad to be able to predict what you are going to do on a Sunday, say, a year from now. Sophia didn't have to come because she was busy sucking up to Anthony's family. It seems the only way out of Sunday dinner is to get engaged! She had even taken a pastizzi she'd made by herself. I hope Anthony's parents don't hold that against her too much.

I yawned, worn out from two evenings of babysitting D and D. Mr. and Mrs. Middleton enjoyed their Friday evening away from the twins so much that they decided to go out again on Saturday. Since I was saving up for a new bra, I couldn't turn down the money. It had been two evenings of hell, but I was a lot closer to my goal. I stared out the rain-streaked car window at wet, yellow leaves lying slick on sidewalks.

Suddenly Hugo said, "So, T, you dating that Phillip guy?"

"Huh?"

Mom immediately turned to stare at me. "What Phillip guy?"

Hugo grinned hugely. He knew Mom couldn't resist the bait.

"Phillip White," I said. "And no, I'm not dating him, Mom." I stuck my tongue out at Hugo. I know it's childish, but that's what he brings out in me.

Horrifying Thought: Did everyone at school think I was hanging out with Phillip? Maybe even, dare I say it, DATING him? I'd be an SN before I knew it.

Understand that I'm not proud of this next thought, but that's the thing about thoughts. They come into our minds unwanted. Even the mean, petty stuff.

Mean Petty Thought: In a way, a really small way, was Phillip partially to blame for getting picked on? Didn't he have some responsibility in this? Really, he just needed a complete Phillip make-over. Dress better, walk without that I'm fair-game-shoot-me shuffle, and definitely lose the briefcase.

"Phillip White. I didn't know he was back in town.

You two used to be such good friends," Mom said. "How nice for you."

Hugo batted his eyes at me and I pinched his thigh. Hard.

"Hey," he yelped.

"You deserved that."

"Stop it," Mom said. "You two are too old to be poking each other."

I retreated into the corner of the back seat and into my thoughts again.

Didn't some of these SNs just set themselves up for this kind of teasing from the ANs?

Take Big Bertha. If she lost some weight, she would not be such a big target for dodge ball—and for Ashleigh.

And Aubrey, that science-geek guy. Well, the first thing he needed to do was change his name. And put himself up for adoption. Any parents who'd name their kid Aubrey were certainly unfit in my eyes. What chance did he have of a normal life with a name like that?

I really am quite good at viewing things from all perspectives. Some people might think it a flip-flop, an indecisive-personality trait, but I see it as being sympathetic to all sides of a situation, a very good characteristic to have if, say, you want to be a hostage negotiator. I wonder, if you were a hostage negotiator, what your boss would say when you told him you couldn't negotiate on a Sunday afternoon because you had a family dinner?

"Why do we have to go to Aunt Grace's anyway?" I

muttered. "You know there's not another single person in my entire school who has to spend every Sunday afternoon with their family. It's so lame."

"I enjoy seeing the family," Hugo said. "I just wish we saw more of them."

I glared at him. "Suck-up idiot," I whispered

"You should be thankful you have a large, loving family to spend a Sunday afternoon with, Teresa," Mom said. "Many children don't even know their grandparents."

I glanced over at Hugo. "Do I have to be thankful for him, too?"

"Don't forget I have a hockey game at three today, Dad," Hugo said smugly. "But, Mom, you and T can stay later. I don't want you to cut your visit short just because of me. I'm sure Nannu could give you a lift home later."

"That's a good idea," Mom said.

I glared at him! Idiot!

He smirked, knowing that I just wanted to get my fill of good food and leave, and his hockey practice would have been the perfect excuse.

"Hey, Dad, can I drive on the way to hockey?"

Mom wouldn't let him drive us all over to Aunt Grace's house.

"I guess," Dad said. "That way you only wipe out *me,* rather than the whole family at once."

"Don't say that, Marshall," Mom scolded. "You're just asking for trouble." Mom has always been a bit superstitious, but lately, since Boo-Boo, she'd been a whole lot more fearful. "You'll bring bad luck on us." She crossed herself once, then twice for good measure. That wasn't the only thing Mom was doing weird. She kept going on food binges. Last week the house was full of nachos, this week, fresh spinach. I preferred the nacho craving.

A few more minutes of driving and it was time for another Sunday Tradition: THE PARKING EVENT.

Every Sunday as we get near Aunt Grace's house, Dad says, "Okay, Fiona, keep your eyes sharp for a parking spot."

Mom peers out the window, pointing out empty spaces, while Dad circles the block a billion times in a hunt for that prime place.

"Global warming, Dad. Car emissions." I yawned again.

Finally Dad found an empty spot, squeezed the car in, and pumped his fist like he'd won a gold medal at the Olympics or something. More weirdly, Mom congratulated him. Hugo and I exchanged grimaces!

Hey, it has nothing to do with us. We didn't pick these people to be our parents.

As soon as we walked into Aunt Grace's, Mom's sisters swept her away to the kitchen and insisted she sit down with her feet up on a chair, jabbering about the expected little *tarbija*, or as we now called her, "Boo-Boo."

I really wished Sophia were here, because it would have driven her nuts that the topic of conversation was babies, not wedding. See. Another mean petty thought. They just come unbidden.

Hearing all the Boo-Boo talk reminded me that I still hadn't told Biff about the baby. Usually we spent every Saturday together, but on Saturday morning I'd sent her this:

E-mail
9:00 a.m.
To: Biff
From: T
Subject: I HAVE PROOF GOD IS SO NOT A WOMAN

> Hi Biff,
> Dying of cramps. Bent over double. Tried standing on my head as I heard that would help, but doesn't. Think I'll stay in today.
> L8R
> T

Lie No. 1: I don't have my period.

I saw the peculiar way Biff looked at me after the Phillip-and-bullies incident and I didn't want to have to explain myself. So rather than face Biff, I took the coward's way out and sent the e-mail. And why should I have to explain myself? Biff sent me an e-mail back saying she hoped I felt better soon. Which made me feel awful for lying. Mind you, she never telephoned to see how I was. Best friends telephone. She should have been concerned.

Hugo and I did a quick tour of the living and dining rooms to see who had come for dinner. There were about twenty people there. The uncles brought Dad a beer and planted him in front of the television for the afternoon. Aunt Grace's was the only place Dad ever went willingly, because no one expected him to make conversation. Here and there, I spotted cousins lurking in corners, some with babies on their knees, but no one I wanted to talk to in a bad way.

"Dorothy didn't land in Oz," Hugo whispered to me. "She landed in Malta. Look at all the Munchkins."

Okay, I hate to admit it, but I actually laughed out loud at that. At five feet ten inches, Hugo was the tallest one there! Dad's English genes were to blame for that, Mom said, as though being five feet ten inches made Hugo a freak. I mean, he is a freak, but not because he's a giant. I'm five foot three, and I'm one of the taller women in the family. They all top out at five feet.

Voices shouted over each other, punctuated by Aunt Anne's shrill laughter (really, she makes hyenas seem lame), were making my head ache, so I decided a quick retreat to the back patio was in order. Unfortunately, I had to go through the kitchen to get to the back door, and I didn't reach it before another Sunday Tradition took place: THE LINGUISTICS LESSON.

Every Sunday Aunt Connie quizzes us kids in Maltese. Except we never learn anything new, because she always asks the same question.

"Who am I?" Aunt Connie asked.

"*Zija Connie*," I'd reply.

"Who him?" she'd ask next, pointing to her husband Mario.

"*Ziju Mario*," I would dutifully tell her.

Maybe she really doesn't know who that hairy little guy is who follows her around.

As usual, she exclaimed over my answers and gave me a hug like I'd done something great. I detached myself from her clutches and went out into the backyard.

My breath came in white clouds and the damp made me wrap my coat tighter, but I didn't mind. It was quiet.

Aunt Grace's garden looked autumn-sad, full of withered, frost-browned stalks with fat beads of water hanging from them. All of it suited my mood. I felt so odd today, like my body was one big sigh. I bet Barbie never had an out-of-sorts day in her whole life. It would be nice to be a plastic person once in a while. Real life needed commercial breaks, like television. Times when you could go and get a drink or a bag of chips, take a bathroom break, and then go back to your life again.

Truth? What was really bothering me was Biff. As I walked around Aunt Grace's garden, I mulled over my feelings and finally decided I was mad at her. Aside from her lack of concern for my well-being, why was she encouraging Phillip to hang out with us? And why didn't she worry about the whole class structure thing at school like I did? And why didn't she have a boy ripping her heart out? Or did she? Was there someone Biff really liked? Surely she would have told me.

I wanted a boyfriend so badly, even I knew I was pathetic. Maybe there was something wrong with me and I should speak to *someone.* Was I normal? Did other girls want boyfriends this badly? I wanted someone to complain about, to agonize over, to walk hand in hand to school with, and to have come up to me in the school hallway and throw an arm around my shoulder and steal a kiss (though the school frowns on PDAs—public displays of affection, for the uninformed). I wanted to have to check with someone before I could make plans. I mean, what girl in her right mind doesn't want to say, "Oh, I'd love to go, but (insert name of boy here) wants me to go to the (insert activity here) with him." And look dismayed, but really be happy inside because she has a BOYFRIEND.

I stopped in front of a statue of the Virgin Mary. In summer it spouts water from her eyes. I mean, it's supposed to do that. It's a fountain, not one of those religious-miracle statues that cries and people flock from miles around to see.

The serene expression on the Virgin's face did nothing to make me feel better. In fact...I looked more closely at her, and stumbled back. She *knew.* She could read the mean, petty thoughts in my head. I shivered, suddenly feeling the cold. And my stomach rumbled. It was just hunger playing with my mind, I decided, and followed my nose inside to the kitchen.

Nanna and the aunts darted between kitchen and dining room with steaming plates of pasta and vegetables and meat. Mom sat at the table, her feet propped up on a stool, picking spinach out of a salad and munching on it. Being "in the family way," she was not to help. Nannu sat beside her. The other men might be in the family room watching sports, but Nannu said he preferred to be surrounded by women, teasing them and saying they were "hens with no heads on."

Then Nanna chimed in. "He's one to talk about us being hens with no heads. The other day, he not find the mail. He put it in the refrigerator. The refrigerator!"

"Oh, Pa," the aunts crowed. They all crowded around him, smothering him with kisses. All except Mom. Her forehead furrowed as she studied Nannu.

Finally they left him alone, and I sat down beside him to show him that I knew how it felt to be the odd man (or woman) out. He put his arm around me, and squeezed. "*Inhobbok.*"

"I love you, too," I replied.

And slowly, my out-of-sorts feeling faded.

I'd be better, I promised God right then and there. I'd give Biff a call as soon as I got home. I'd tell her about the baby, though it would mean . . .

Lie No. 2: "We just found out today."

Please forgive me for that lie, God, but otherwise Biff's feelings would be hurt, which I think is worse than lying.

And, I went on silently, *I'll be nicer to Big Bertha. I*

might even say hello to Aubrey. And Phillip—well, I'll try to be civil, God, but don't expect any miracles. I'm not a saint.

Nanna noticed the rash on my arms. I told Mom it'd spread to my chest. She was horrified. It's a nasty-looking, red, blistery rash. She was also guilt-ridden: a good mother would have noticed a nasty, blistery rash on her daughter's arms. Mom got all teary (hormones, the aunts told her) and I said not to worry about it. She'd had a lot on her mind. Nannu said he and Nanna would take me to the medical walk-in clinic after school tomorrow so Mom didn't have to take time off work. I'm glad, as it has been awfully itchy.

j is For jerK

Biff and I are friends again. As soon as I got home Sunday night (quite an adventure, with Nannu driving the wrong way on a one-way street and Nanna and Mom screaming!) I phoned and told her about Boo-Boo. And yes, I did use Lie No. 2. It was worth any punishment that might come my way to not hurt Biff's feelings. She was very excited. And this morning, wonder of wonders, Phillip wasn't waiting at the corner for us. Dental appointment, Biff said. I cheered and told Biff I'd missed just the two of us walking together.

"Phillip's going through a rough time with his dad leaving and the move," Biff said. "He's having trouble fitting in. It doesn't hurt to be nice to him. And he likes you, T, so be kind."

Biff being so understanding and kind and thoughtful

made me feel like the worst person in the world, and reminded me of my promise to the HP to be nice to everyone. And you know, I would be except for those dratted mean, petty thoughts.

Mean, Petty Thought: I couldn't help wishing all of Phillip's teeth would fall out so that he would have dental appointments every morning. In fact, they should fit him for dentures.

First Fright: Dentures.

I was eight years old and Grandpa T had died, so Grandma T stayed a couple of nights with us. In my bed.

I walked in to get my pajamas (I was sleeping on the couch) just as Grandma T reached into her mouth and took out her teeth and dropped them in a teacup. She couldn't have shocked me more if she'd taken out her intestines. I screamed and screamed while Mom explained about dentures and Grandma T scolded me for my foolishness. I had nightmares of giant teeth chasing me for weeks.

"You're lopsided again," Biff said.

I shifted the sock and winced. The bra straps were losing their elasticity from all the tugging of the sock, and my skin was getting raw from the friction. Between that and my rash, I was an itchy mess.

"I have enough money now for a new bra," I told Biff. "And I have the scars from babysitting D and D to prove it. Maybe we can go to the mall on the weekend." ACK! I just remembered.

"I have to go to the doctor this afternoon with Nanna and Nannu!" I told Biff. I clutched her arm. "What if I have to take off my bra? The doctor will see the sock! And," I shook Biff's arm, "I have a thong on. I can't wear a thong and a sock-bra to the doctor!" I wailed. "It's not decent." I cannot believe that underwear was causing me so much anxiety. I cannot believe that I just sounded like Grandma T. *Not decent?*

"She's just going to look at your arms," Biff said soothingly.

"I guess you're right. Why do we have to keep our boobs inside these bras anyway?" I grumbled.

"It is men's way of keeping women symbolically contained," Biff said. "All through the ages, until the 1960s when women burned their bras, men had control over women's clothing. Men feared women, so they bound and shackled the symbols of womanhood to make themselves feel better."

Boy, it was good to be back with Biff.

I gave my bra a final poke as we went up the sidewalk to the school door. "Do you think guys obsess about their, you-know-whats?"

We passed a group of ANs standing just off the school lawn, a white cloud of cigarette smoke hanging over their heads. I glanced sideways and saw Adam in the middle. I didn't know he smoked. It made him seem sort of … bad. I decided I liked bad.

"I hear most guys keep rulers in their nightstand," Biff said.

"Why?" I asked.

Biff rolled her eyes at me. We opened the heavy doors and went to our lockers. As I got my books out for class, it finally hit me. Rulers … guys.

First Reaction: Eewww.
Second Reaction: Snicker.

"I get it," I yelled down the hall to Biff. She grinned back.

Mental Note to Self: Never borrow a ruler from a guy.

"Hey."

I looked over my shoulder, and there was AAA. I turned beet red.

"I just wanted to make sure you were okay from Greg bumping you the other day," he said.

OMIGAWD! He actually worried about me. Like a real boyfriend would.

"I'm … I'm fine," I stammered.

"What happened to your accent?" he asked. "I thought you were English."

"Oh, I speak Canadian, too. And also … um … Maltese," I stammered. "Like, my brother is a pain in the *hamar*. That's Maltese for 'ass.' Though it means donkey ass, not butt ass." I could actually HEAR Biff's eyes roll behind me. "I'm half-Maltese. That's a tiny island in the Mediterranean. But my Grandma T is English. Blimey, bloody," I babbled on.

"Multilingual. Cute. Well, I'm glad you're okay," AAA said, and with a smile, headed down the hall, taking my heart with him.

"Cheerio," I called.

"You're multilingual?" Biff demanded.

"Hey, I didn't know either until I started talking. It must be like a gift or something," I said. "Did you hear him? I'm cute!"

I heard a locker slam beside me. Phillip. I hadn't even seen him come in.

"Hi, Teresa." Ashleigh waved as she passed. "See you in homeroom."

"G'day, mate," I replied.

"That's Australian," Biff said.

Omigawd! I really was multilingual. I could be a translator for the government, and as it came so easily to me, I wouldn't even have to go to college or university. I could just start working and getting paid humongous amounts of money.

Phillip banged his locker again.

Biff studied me. "So when did Ashleigh start talking to you?"

"In gym class. She also put me on her dodge ball team. She's actually not all that bad," I said.

"You do know she wants something."

"What?"

"Ashleigh. She isn't being friendly because she likes you," Biff said.

Another bang from Phillip's locker. Annoying.

"Could you stop doing that?" I shouted at him.

"Sorry," he said, though it came out as "schorry" because his mouth was frozen. "I didn't mean to interrupt you and your *schpecial friensh*."

"Well, that's rather insulting," I said to Biff, ignoring Phillip. "Why couldn't Ashleigh like me?"

"I'm not saying you're not likeable," Biff explained. "It's just you're not likeable to Ashleigh and her kind. She uses people."

"You're likeable to me," Phillip said.

I guess he'd got over whatever was making him mad.

"You're drooling. It's disgusting," I told him.

Phillip wiped his mouth on his sleeve.

"Seriously, Biff, she's not all that bad once you get to know her." I took a deep sniff. "Do you smell that?"

"What? Cigarette smoke? It stinks," Biff said.

"It's a wonderful stink," I sighed. "It's AAA's stink. I love it."

"Yeah, right," Biff said. She walked off, not waiting to go to homeroom together.

"I think *shesh upshet* with you," Phillip said.

"She'll get over it. Get lost."

I was almost an AN and I didn't want Phillip screwing it up for me.

"You know what, Teresa, you *shure* have changed," Phillip said. He turned and headed down the hall.

I stared after them. Well, of course I'd changed. People are supposed to grow and change. Not just stay losers, like Phillip. Why do I never think to say these things when people are around?

Biff was just being snotty and all high-and-mighty, and Phillip, well, he was just being a jerk. In fact, they were both being jerks. They didn't want to see me happy. Biff was probably jealous that Ashleigh was being friendly with me and Adam was my almost boyfriend. Okay, that was just a bitchy comment that I really didn't believe … much.

Maybe Biff was afraid that if I had a boyfriend or moved up to the AN class I wouldn't be friends with her anymore? I'd assure her on the way home after school that she'd always be my best friend no matter how many boyfriends I had, though I'd remind her of our pact—boyfriends come before girlfriends. No hard feelings.

My feet floated down the school hall toward homeroom as I began making AAA plans, like helping him quit smoking. It might make him look a bit bad, but it could ultimately give him lung cancer and kill him. Yes, I'd help Adam change his bad-boy ways and he'd be incredibly grateful to me. We'd hold hands everywhere we walked. We were going to be the best boyfriend-girlfriend ever. Tenth grade was shaping up to be the best year of my life.

k is For kiss = bewsA
(Maltese)

I got cramps for real, and they were bad. Obviously, the HP is punishing me for lying to Biff last weekend and telling her I had cramps when I didn't.

At least it was Saturday morning and I could stay in bed. And I planned to stay in bed the entire day and have a huge self-pity party. That, and the fact that Biff hadn't even called last night to make our weekend plans, was what was keeping me in. For a week that had started out so well, it sure turned disastrous fast.

My Week

Monday: Nanna and Nannu took me to the doctor. You would have thought that I was going for major surgery, the way they helped me into the car and tucked a blanket over my legs. That was after Nannu sat outside the school, blowing the car horn about a billion times, while Nanna stood beside it, waving her arms and calling "Teresa" at the top of her voice. The entire smoking pit was laughing. That's about three months' worth of embarrassment.

At the walk-in clinic, Nanna insisted on coming in with me despite me telling her I was fine on my own. I did, though, take a stand on Nannu coming in too.

So the doctor looked at my arms (and only my arms, thank goodness—remember sock-bra, thong?) and asked if I had handled anything unusual before the rash started.

I thought way, way back to the first time the rash appeared and remembered the only *unusual* thing I'd been handling. But how could I tell the doctor with Nanna there? So I hummed and hawed a bit, then whispered, "condom" and started to giggle and turn red.

"Cotton?" Nanna said. "How could she be allergic to cotton? She wear cotton all the time."

"A condom." The doctor enunciated loudly for Nanna's benefit.

"On a banana, for practice, in Health class," I added quickly. I didn't want the doctor to think I was one of *those* girls.

Translation: Those girls = "skanks."

The doctor's eyebrows shot up under her bangs.

"Why you put cotton on a banana?" Nanna asked, completely bewildered.

"Though why they use bananas I have no idea. And never peel it first. I learned that the hard way. My banana broke..." I was really babbling here.

Contact dermatitis, the doctor diagnosed, trying really hard not to laugh. An allergy to latex. Well, there's my life over before it even started. I'll never be able to have sex. Nanna might get that nun in the family after all. I mean, who wants contact dermatitis *there*!

· · · · ·

I crawled out of the bed and headed to the bathroom. There were no pads in the cupboard under the sink. I listened at the top of the stairs and heard Sophia in the kitchen talking to Mom about the wedding. Obviously Sophia's little hissy fit about Boo-Boo was over.

I tiptoed into Sophia's room and, using only my pinky, opened her closet door. I should have worn gloves! She probably had a fingerprint kit. I carefully extracted two blue-wrapped packages from a sanitary napkin box, closed the closet, and worked my way backwards out of the room, my bare toes raking the carpet as I went to cover my foot-prints. A spy couldn't have done better. I headed to the bathroom with my pilfered booty.

Secret: I'm scared to use tampons. It creeps me out how you put them in. Yuck!

Back in my room, I propped Barbie and Ken on the pillow beside me. When one has bad cramps, one needs all the support one can get.

· · · · ·

Tuesday: A tiff with Biff again because she thinks I'm dumb. Well, I might be stupid, but I'm certainly not dumb.

Dumb: You don't have knowledge of something.

Stupid: You have the knowledge of something, but you disregard it and do something stupid anyway.

Reason for Tiff with Biff: She keeps warning me that Ashleigh's sudden interest in me is for a purpose, and that Ashleigh will use me for something and that something won't be good. I'm not dumb; I know that, but it still hurts that Biff can't even think for one minute that Ashleigh might like me for ME! Is that so hard to believe? Well, yes. But I still feel hurt. Besides, this "using" idea could work both ways. I could use Ashleigh to my advantage. She was a doorway to opportunity. A doorway leading directly to AAA. A doorway I had every intention of going through.

Wednesday: Dodge ball again. Hid behind Big Bertha again. Conscience bugging me. Hate my conscience.

Thursday: Babysat D and D for an hour after school. Those boys are definitely displaying serial killer traits. I told Mom and she said not to be so silly, that they are just ordinary six-year-old boys. I hope she feels like that when she wakes up one night to find them standing over her with a knife!

Friday: Tried to explain to Biff the advantages of being Ashleigh's friend. Said I would introduce her to Ashleigh and she could enjoy the advantages also. Biff said, "That's big of you." At first I thought she was grateful. Now I think she was being sarcastic.

• • • • •

I explained the entire Ashleigh situation to Barbie, and she suggested I make a list of all the possible things Ashleigh could want. Ken suggested he and Barbie get naked. I tapped him sharply on the head with my pencil.

List of What Ashleigh Wants:
1. Help with homework. (Not likely, since I'm not that great a student. She should have picked Biff.)
2. She likes my clothing style and wants help with hers. (Yeah, right!)

I chewed the end of the pencil. I'm really good at making lists, but this time I was stumped. What did I have that Ashleigh wanted?
3. (Ken's addition) She's a lesbian and is hitting on you.

I tapped Ken on the head again, but then gave in and

undressed Barbie and him. Anything to shut him up. Then the three of us sat in silence. I chewed my pencil. Ken pondered his smooth crotch and, occasionally, Barbie's nippleless boobs. I took pity on him a second time and drew nipples on Barbie. But they looked like bullseyes so I erased them.

Note to the Dumb: Not only does marker not come off plastic, but pencil does not erase well from plastic either.

I resumed chewing the pencil, and discovered I'd flipped it around and was gnawing on the wrong end! Crapola. I was done for.

I yelled downstairs to Mom: "Can you get lead poisoning from chewing a pencil?"

Mom said, "Why are you chewing a pencil?"

"What about the eraser? Can you get poisoned from the eraser?"

"Oh, for Pete's sake," Sophia shouted back. "Why don't you just take arsenic and get it over with."

Really, she is such a b-t-h. I slammed my door shut and resumed my list.

4. Ashleigh has had a religious conversion and is being nice to all people no matter what their place is in the hierarchy of the high school class system.

Barbie immediately scoffed at that.

"So, Miss Know-It-All," I said, "what does Ashleigh want?"

Barbie tipped over toward Ken. Nope, still didn't get it. Maybe if I thought about something else it'd come to me. I'd think about kissing.

Now, I'd done a great deal of research on the proper kissing technique. My sources were magazine articles and afternoon soaps. They really go at it on those soaps. And I'd given and received a few pecks at parties. So I had the basics down. Except I'd never had a long, deep kiss with someone I was crazy about. But the ways things were going… that might change. So, I decided to practice on my forearm.

Kissing Procedure (Mostly Theoretical)
1. Look deep into the other person's eyes. (But not so deep that he thinks you're a staring weirdo.)
2. Tilt head opposite way to the other person's tilt. (You can't both tilt the same way. Reason in No. 3.)
3. Watch noses. (Nothing is more awkward than giving your guy a bloody nose.)
4. Open lips slightly. This is a very delicate area. You need to open your lips enough so that they are soft and the guy gets the idea he isn't getting a buff from his mother, but not open so much that he thinks you're a slut.
5. If you really like the guy, you can touch the tip of his tongue with yours. (If you REALLY like the guy, you can try to find his tonsils. That's just a little joke.)
6. Onions are a definite NN (no-no), as are garlic and

stinky sausage. Oh yes, and lettuce stuck between your teeth is definitely a turn-off.

I'd just laid a wet one on my forearm when Mom came in with a duster. She took one look at me sucking my arm, then at the mess called my room, and turned around muttering "I don't want to know" under her breath.

"Hey, Mom." I called her back. "Do you remember your high school days?" I was curious as to what impact high school would have on my adult life.

"Well, some things about them," Mom said. She got a faraway look in her eyes. "I remember this one time—"

"Oh, that's okay," I interrupted. "I don't want to *hear* about those days. I just wondered if once you got old, you remembered stuff like that."

"I'm not old," Mom said huffily.

"Well, Nannu forgets stuff all the time," I pointed out to her.

"Nannu is thirty years older than me! He's my father. Your grandfather."

"Well, it won't be long before you'll be his age and you'll be putting the mail in the fridge too," I said. "Don't worry, Mom. I'll make sure we find a nice nursing home for you. Hugo will pay for it."

"Clean your room. Today! No going out until it's done. See, there are some advantages to being old—I can tell you what to do." Mom left.

I was in no hurry to clean my room. Biff obviously

wasn't going to call. I don't know what is wrong with her these days. She takes everything I say the wrong way.

I decided to get back to my List of What Ashleigh Wants. Looking down, I saw that I'd doodled Hugo's name.

Hugo! What did I have that Ashleigh wanted? A brother. Hugo. Omigawd! It was like ghostwriting. Maybe I was a natural medium. I could open my own psychic hotline and make oodles of cash.

And Barbie had known. That was why she'd tipped toward Ken. She had psychic powers too. Or maybe she was possessed. Dolls get possessed. Whatever! Well, I'd get Ashleigh her Hugo, if she got me my AAA.

The telephone rang, and Dad called up that it was for me. Biff! Wait until she heard about Ashleigh and Hugo.

I ran into Mom and Dad's room and picked up the extension, but it wasn't Biff.

"Hi, Teresa," a voice chirped. "It's me, Ashleigh. The Glams and I were wondering if you wanted to come to the mall with us this afternoon."

Omigawd! Me? The Glams? The mall? Breathe deeply. I strived for a don't-give-a-crapola reply, "Yeah, sure. What time?"

"I'll call you back and let you know," Ashleigh said. "Do you have a cell phone?"

Silence.

"Minutes," I said, my mind working furiously.

"Huh?"

"I ran out of minutes. You know. I need to buy some more. So just call me on this line," I said. I heard the beep that signalled another call was coming in.

I quickly said goodbye and hit the flash button.

"Hi, T." It was Biff. "Sorry I didn't call before, but Mom made me go to Grandma's right after school yesterday. We stayed overnight. I didn't know so I couldn't tell you sooner."

Uh-oh.

"So, what do you want to do this afternoon? Get your new bra?"

If I told Biff the truth, would she understand that I didn't want to remember my high school days as the worst days of my life? Would she understand how badly I wanted AAA as a boyfriend? Somehow I didn't think she would.

Lie No. 3: "Gee, Mom's making me stay in today. She says I have to clean my room."

Please note that this isn't really a lie because Mom did say I had to clean my room before I went out.

"Do you want me to come over and help?" Biff asked. "It'd go faster with the two of us and then we could go out."

Lie No. 4: "No, she says I have to do it myself. You know, stuff about responsibility. I also have to help clean the rest of the house today. We're all pitching in, you know, what with her delicate condition and all."

I am a horrible person. This is a real lie and I used my mom's "delicate condition" (Grandma T's phrase for pregnancy) for my own purposes.

"T!" Sophia's shrill voice came through the wall between our rooms. "You were in my room again!"

"Sophia's coming to kill me. I'll call you tonight, bye."

I sprinted back to my room, slammed the door shut and heaved my dresser in front of it.

A second later, the door crashed against the dresser. "I know it was you," Sophia shouted through the crack.

"You're wasting your talents in insurance," I shouted back, confident she couldn't get past the dresser. "You should be a spy. You know, Anthony is going to be in your room all the time soon. Are you going to fingerprint him?"

Okay, never underestimate the strength of an enraged sister. Inch by inch the dresser moved and the door opened. I pushed back with all my might and started screaming for Mom. Sure, it's the coward's way out to have your mommy save you, but what the heck, I was willing to be a coward. I didn't want to be like Grandma T and keep my teeth in a cup.

12

L is For Love And Lust

It's very important that you know the difference between Love and Lust, and that you don't accidentally mistake one for the other. Otherwise you could run into BIG problems. It's actually very simple. Love is good and Lust is bad.

Dictionary Definition of Love: 1. Intense affection. 2. A feeling of attraction resulting from sexual desire. 3. Enthusiasm or fondling ... (oops, I meant fondness) such as love of music. (Or in my case, love of AAA.)

And then there are all kinds of other words with love in them, such as *love*bird, *love*lorn (that's what I am without AAA), *love*making, *lover*, *love* seat (a.k.a. small couch.) Put them all together in a sentence and you'd get:

I love lovemaking with my lover (AAA) *on the love seat.*

Dictionary Definition of Lust: 1. Intense and often excessive or unrestrained sexual desire. 2. An intense desire.

The Church is always telling us teens to say no until you're married, when the priests suddenly change their minds and want you to say yes, yes, yes and have lots of sex which leads to lots of babies. I think the Church would prefer that people married in lust rather than in love.

Now substitute *lust* for *love* in my sentence above. (The *lust* seat. Isn't that funny?) I'm so confused now. I think I love AND lust Adam.

One thing I'm certain of is that I *love* shopping!

· · · · ·

The doors to the mall parted, and I followed Ashleigh and the Glams into what I imagine heaven to be.

Heaven: Pearly gates open majestically and Saint Peter welcomes me to—THE MALL. He hands me a huge bag of money and tells me there's lots more where that came from.

I stopped just inside the mall doors and sniffed deeply of the MALL AROMA: Popcorn, salami (from the sandwich place), perfume, and the heady scent of stuff, stuff, stuff to buy.

Note to Self: Suggest to air-freshener people that they bottle and sell mall aroma, with 90 percent of the profit going to me because it was my idea.

It doesn't get any better than this. Me. ANs. The mall. People seeing me with ANs. Pink lip gloss that I borrowed from Sophia. I mean, I couldn't go to the mall with just plain lips. These are real memories I'm building here, not those dumb museum, Grand-Canyon-vacation memories Dad says I'll look back on with pleasure in years to come. Yeah, right.

I wanted to go out and walk back into the mall, just so I could get that great feeling again.

Cramps forgotten, I'd cleaned my room in record time after Ashleigh's call. Even Mom had to admit that it was a good job. Of course, she hadn't looked in my closet. Actually, I really hoped she wouldn't look in my closet. The stuff piled up in there could come crashing down on her and her "delicate condition."

How It Feels to Be Popular: You toss your hair around. You squeal at a great purse in a store window. You take wider steps when you walk and you thrust your chest out and keep your head up. You open your mouth to laugh. You roll your eyes at each other when you see someone's pant legs flapping around their ankles. You make a bit of a spectacle of yourself in stores and in front of guys, though you pretend you don't see the guys, who pretend they don't see you—so there's a lot of non-looking looking going on. In short, it feels GREAT!

And that great feeling turned me into a giddy clown. But that was okay because the Glams needed a humorous addition. I mean, they had dumb Melanie, Kara and her *brains*, "Yes-girl" Stephanie, and the all-powerful Queen Ashleigh. But no clown. I took to the role with enthusiasm.

In one store I wrapped a fur stole around my neck and pranced up and down aisles, nose in the air, speaking snobby England-English like Grandma T. In the toy store I pulled a line of quacking ducks behind me, and in the music store I danced wildly with headphones on, to music that only I could hear. Ashleigh nearly peed herself she laughed so hard.

We sprayed each other with perfume testers and turned our hands into rainbows with different-colored lipstick samples.

I had planned to use my babysitting money to buy a new air-bra. Instead, in my new, outrageous, generous persona, I treated the Glams to fries and drinks. And I also bought a really great (though expensive) purse that Ashleigh said made me look really cool. I figured, why not? I could always keep stuffing a sock into my old bra, but when would I ever get another chance to break into the Glams?

After the high-fat pig-out, we went into a plus-size women's store. I held a giant-cupped bra (must have been a gazillion ZZ cup) up to my chest and we all giggled. Then I pulled a pair of size 22W underpants over my jeans. Laughing, I turned around—and there was Big

Bertha with her mother. At the same time, a sales clerk came striding toward me from the opposite direction. I was trapped.

"Take those off," the sales clerk ordered. "I could have you arrested for shoplifting."

Everyone in the store turned to stare at me, including Big Bertha and her mother. But the Glams? They were nowhere to be seen.

I hopped on one foot, then the other, nearly falling flat on my face as I stepped out of the underpants. Face red, I handed them to the clerk.

"We can't resell these because you opened the package," she said coldly. "You'll have to buy them. That will be $8.99."

I rooted through my purse, counting all the change I could find, but I was four dollars short. "I'm so ... sorry," I stammered. "I can go home and get the money."

"I'm afraid I'll have to call security."

OMIGAWD! I was going to jail. I'd seen movies about women's jail. The first thing they did was make you strip off all your clothes while they hosed you down and sprayed you with lice powder. They'd see the sock stuffed in my bra! I'd be the lamest person in the prison.

"Here." Big Bertha came up beside me and pushed a five-dollar bill into my hand.

I didn't know what to do. Big Bertha wasn't supposed to rescue ME, but on the other hand, I didn't want to expose my sock-bra in jail.

"Thanks. I'll pay you back at school. I promise," I muttered. I blinked back tears of humiliation as the sales clerk rang up the underpants and put them into a bag. I grabbed it and ran out of the store.

Outside, a hand latched onto my arm and jerked me to one side of the store's glass doors. My heart stopped. Seriously, it did. I felt it skip a beat, because I was sure it was the mall security guard. It was Ashleigh.

"What happened?" she asked.

The Glams crowded around me. My legs felt shaky. At first I was mad. The Glams had bailed on me. Some friends they were. But they were patting my back, and Kara was giving me a hug and I was one of them again, so I forgave them. I opened the bag and showed the underpants. "The sales clerk made me buy them."

"The bitch," Ashleigh said.

"Yeah," I agreed weakly. "The bitch."

I didn't say anything about Big Bertha coming to my rescue and lending me the money to save me from going to jail. Fright over, I began mimicking the sales clerk's haughty manner. That's when I saw Biff walking up the mall toward us, alone. I ducked behind Melanie, but it was too late. Biff had seen me. She came right up to us, looked over the Glams, then tilted her head to one side and studied me, not saying a word.

"It's not what you think," I said.

"Really? What I think is that you ditched me so you

could go out with Ashleigh and her girly gang. What I'm thinking is that you lied to me."

Okay. It was what she was thinking.

"You suck," Biff said. She turned and walked away and was soon lost in the crowd.

"What was that all about?" Ashleigh asked. Then before I could answer, she shrugged. "Who cares? She's weird. Let's go." She linked her arm in mine.

Surrounded by the Glams made me feel marginally better, but I couldn't get back Outrageous Teresa. Everything felt a bit flat now, and my cramps came back. I felt really bad that I'd let Biff just walk away.

"I'm going to go home," I said. "I have to babysit tonight." I looked glumly at the new purse. Too bad I couldn't wear it on my chest.

"There's a party next Saturday night," Ashleigh said. "You should come. Lots of people will be there." She listed names, but I was still feeling sorry for myself and not paying attention until I heard, "Adam."

"Adam?" I asked. I hoped they couldn't hear my heart thundering. Between this and it skipping beats, it's a wonder I'm not dead from a heart attack.

"Adam, and Greg."

Omigawd! AAA!

"Your brother can come too. Will you tell him about it?" Ashleigh added.

Aha. Barbie was right! Ashleigh had it bad for Hugo.

• • • • •

Back home before I headed out to babysit, I typed up an e-mail.

E-mail
5:37 p.m.
To: Biff
From: T
Subject: This afternoon at the mall

> Biff, I can explain! It's a biological problem over which I have no control. (Also a great anthropology study topic.)
> Please call or e-mail me back. I'm really sorry!
> L8R
> T

But I deleted it before I could hit *send*. Maybe I hadn't acted like a best friend, but what right did Biff have to look me over like I was one of her anthropology projects? She was just jealous that I was now popular and she wasn't. She should be supportive and happy for me, but instead she'd ruined my fabulous day. I didn't need to apologize.

I gathered up a pen and paper to take with me to the Middletons. Hopefully D and D would give me two minutes' peace. It was vital that I make a pre-party planning list. My head buzzed with plans, and Biff was forgotten.

m is For misery AnD money

(You can never have enough.
Money, that is. You can have enough misery.)

Sunday morning. There was so much to do before the party next weekend. I didn't know how I was going to cope with everything. I also had a huge History project on World War II due in a couple of weeks. The project was about the impact of the war on the general population of a country, including economic and emotional factors. I have discovered that the secret to not letting life overwhelm you is to prioritize your time. Here was my priority list for the next week:

1. Prepare for party (huge, and therefore number one).
2. History Project.

I could do History any old time. (Little joke: "old time."

Get it?) How difficult could my project be? Everyone knows how World War II worked out. It's history. It wasn't going to change. On the other hand, if I messed up the party, I'd be a social outcast for the entire rest of my life!

Barbie, Ken, and I brainstormed.

Party Preparation List: (in no particular order)
1. A crash course in English (England-English).
2. Buy new bra. (Problem: need more money.)
3. Practice clever things to say to AAA other than *ga-ga-ga*.
4. Flatten frizzy hair. (Borrow/steal Sophia's straightener?)
5. Convince Mom to let me go to the party.
6. Convince Hugo to go to the party, which will help convince Mom to let me go to the party.
7. Decide what to wear. (Barbie pointed out that I'd better schedule two days for that, and perhaps a third for a shopping trip should the need arise. I completely agree.)
8. Get heart tattoo with AAA in middle. (Tiny, just above my butt crack.)
9. Bum crunches.

I crossed out number eight. Mom would never let me do it. Plus I'm not that keen on needles sticking into my skin.

I did, though, substitute another entry for number eight. "Pay back Big Bertha!" True, it wasn't part of the party prep, but it had to be done. There goes another five dollars of my precious earnings, and all I had to show for it was a humongous pair of women's underwear stuck in the back of my dresser drawer. That was okay. I was in love.

How It Feels to Be In Love: Absolutely miserable. Your stomach is in knots. Your palms sweat. Your hearing goes. Your brain turns to mush. You walk around under a cloud of misery all the time. It's the absolute best!

Reviewing the list, I could see a basic problem with numbers two and seven. Money, currency, dollars, coins. At first glance, money appears to be merely a piece of paper or a handful of metal. It's so much more. It's lip gloss, cool jeans, great boots, a coat, sweaters, air-bra, hair mousse, movies, soft drinks, fries. If I were a Buddhist monk, money wouldn't be of any importance. (Mind you, how much expense is involved in wearing an orange robe day in and day out, a robe that isn't even properly fitted? One size fits all.) But I'm a Catholic. I need money.

Teenagers and money go hand in hand. Nannu obviously understands that as he is always slipping us kids "a little something." The truth is that I have been on a quest for financial gain for many years. At least since I was ten. Back then I wanted the super-duper Barbie Dream House. I have never wanted anything so badly in my life (other than AAA) as that Dream House. Advertising bombarded me. It told me that if I had the super-duper Barbie Dream House, I'd be set for life. I got the house for Christmas, but then I saw the super-duper Barbie convertible. Barbie and

I both lusted after that car. So we got the car. And then there was stuff Ken wanted...and so it goes. I am never satisfied. Some might look upon this as a character flaw, but I prefer to look on it as a strength. I am not willing to just settle.

Mom and Dad give Hugo and me a pittance of a weekly allowance. I mean seriously, it barely covers my *necessities*, as I see them. Mom and Dad insist we buy our own *luxuries*, as they see them. Over the years there has been some controversy as to the definition of *luxury* versus *necessity*. For example:

Me: Lip gloss—necessity. Important for self-esteem.
Mom and Dad: Lip gloss—luxury. Too young for make-up anyway.

Me: Cell phone—necessity. Keeping up with my peers.
Mom and Dad: Cell phone—luxury. And worry about brain damage.

I think it's all subjective, like some people saying money is the root of all evil. I say it's the freeway to happiness. But back to my money problem: the solution was simple, if distressing. I'd have to bite the bullet and babysit D and D and hope they wouldn't kill me.

In the meantime, I needed to work on numbers five and six before I could proceed to any further items on my list.

Once permission was given, I had every confidence the rest of my list would fall into place.

I wandered down to the kitchen. Mom dashed about scrambling eggs, making coffee, and dropping bread into the toaster, hurrying to get breakfast before we left for church. No time like the present to suck up. I quickly ran over and grabbed the frying pan from her hands.

"Let me do that," I said, then yelped and dropped the pan on the floor. Metal handle, heat, no oven mitt. Mom looked at the yellow mess on the floor. Good thing she was over that upchucking thing.

"Sorry. I'll clean it up," I said as I ran cold water over my burned palm. "You sit down and put your feet up. You really should rest more."

I scraped eggs from the floor back into the pan and set it on the stove to heat up again. "There. No one needs to know where that was." I laughed.

Mom sank into a chair, a stunned expression on her face.

"Mom," I said, "have I told you how great you look? You have that pregnant-woman glow about you." I'd heard that comment on a television show. "And Boo-Boo is really starting to show," I added.

That comment I picked up from Aunt Grace last Sunday, as the sisters piled their discarded maternity clothes into Mom's arms. It seems when you're pregnant, you suddenly are in need of charity. People were cleaning out their closets and dumping their unwanted stuff on Mom. Dad should just put a big box outside the house for people to drop their junk off.

"You sit there and rest. I'll set the table for breakfast." Was this overkill? I stole a look at Mom's face. Still stunned-looking, but not suspicious. Good.

"You know, Mom." I carefully lined up four forks and knives next to plates, except Hugo's. I threw flatware in the general direction of where he sat. I don't know why we even give him cutlery. He just inhales his food. "Next Saturday, there's this party, a school-pride party. Oh, I don't mean a gay-pride thing…"

Sophia wandered into the room in her pajamas, yawning hugely. She headed directly to the coffee machine and grabbed a mug and the pot. She didn't notice that the coffee was still running out onto the element, spitting and hissing.

"I think I'll go with red roses, not white ones," she said, pouring brown liquid into a cup. "Anthony and I were talking last night and we think red is better for a winter wedding than—"

"It's a school-spirit thing," I yelled, drowning out Sophia.

"I was talking here," Sophia said.

"Well, I was talking here first, before you even arrived," I protested. "You think that everyone is just sitting around waiting for you to talk wedding? Well, we have lives too. And you're making a mess of that coffee machine!"

"Girls," Mom said, then more loudly, "Girls!"

"Teresa, you go first since you were here before Sophia," she said when we'd quieted down.

"First of all, Sophia, you shouldn't upset Mom when she's in a delicate condition," I began.

"Teresa..." Mom's voice held a warning note.

I buttered toast for Mom, heaped on strawberry jam (her latest craving) and put it in front of her, then spooned eggs onto a plate and pushed them toward Sophia. "Here, sit down and eat the breakfast I made you," I said sweetly.

Mom raised her eyebrows at me. I winked. We both knew where those eggs had been.

"Anyway, Mother" (I think *Mother* sounds more mature than *Mom*—I mean, like *I'm* more mature, not Mom is more mature), "I really think I should go to show my support for my school."

"Let me talk it over with Dad," Mom began.

"That will take forever," I complained. "You know Dad doesn't talk."

I poured myself a bowl of cereal. "How are those eggs?" I asked Sophia.

"Surprisingly good, considering you made them," she replied.

"Secret ingredient," I said. Floor dirt.

Hugo wandered in. "I got checked at hockey last night, Mom." He pulled up his T-shirt and showed a large purple bruise on his ribs. He pressed his fingers to it and winced, though you could see he was quite proud of its size. "I think I'll stay home from church this morning. Maybe Dad will go with you in my place."

Yeah, like Dad would go. He only attends church on special occasions, mostly because he hates the part where he's expected to shake hands with people when the priest tells us to wish each other "peace." Instead, Dad studies the ceiling of the church and pushes his own hands deep into his pockets. Mom says it's embarrassing, and she has to be extra-friendly to make up for him. He says he doesn't want strangers' germs on his hands.

"Okay. Sophia can take your place," Mom said.

Because Sophia is older, she can usually decide for herself whether or not to go to church.

"After all," Mom continued. "you can't get married in a church you don't show your face at."

"Just us women," I said heartily.

"Have some eggs, Hugo," I offered. "There was something I was supposed to tell you. Now what was it…?"

I made a show of screwing up my forehead and pursing my lips. I frowned and then I did a lightbulb moment like I'd just remembered something. Give me the Oscar now and forget the rest of the nominees.

"Oh, right. Ashleigh Harcourt said there was a school-spirit party next Saturday night and that you're invited."

Hugo nodded his head, but didn't stop eating.

I crossed my fingers underneath the table. "We should go, don't you think? For school spirit, I mean."

I'm not sure how crossing fingers cancels out a lie. I think it's like absolution.

"And all the school sports teams are going. So you'll want to be there representing the hockey team."

Hugo shoveled in eggs and toast. Obviously, injured ribs didn't hurt the appetite.

"So, are you going to go?" I asked.

"Anthony and I decided we're canceling the white flowers and going with red," Sophia said to Mom. (Yeah, like Anthony decided anything!) "Of course," Sophia continued, "that means I'll have to change my bouquet, and the maid of honor dress will have to be changed. That red isn't going to go well with the green."

"Red sounds like the right choice," I told Sophia. Anything to get rid of that puke-green dress.

"So, Hugo," I turned back to him. "Are you going to the party?"

"Dunno," he mumbled, spraying toast crumbs all over the table.

"You really should. It would show school spirit. I think there might even be some teachers and your coach going." As all my fingers were crossed, I now had to resort to my toes. "And she invited me, too. I don't know. I guess I'll go. I mean, we should all show school spirit. So, are you going?"

"And Mom," Sophia went on, "maybe you could carry a big purse, so *that* won't be too obvious." Sophia waved in the direction of Mom's stomach. "Or perhaps a poncho?"

Hugo pushed away his plate, and a few minutes later I heard the computer boot up. He is *so* annoying. Fine. I would decide for him. He's going.

"So is that okay with you, Mom?" I asked.

"Is what okay?" Mom looked harassed trying to follow two conversations. "We can't very well cancel all those dresses at this late date, Sophia. We're sticking with the white. And I'm not wearing a poncho. Giving birth is nothing to be ashamed of."

"The school spirit event next Saturday night. Hugo said I could go with him, so that should be okay, right?"

"Yes, I guess so. If Hugo will look out for you and it's a school event."

"Fabuloso!" I dumped my plate in the sink. Numbers five and six accomplished.

I was on such a roll I decided to work on number one. And there was only one place to learn England-English.

"You know, Mom, we see Nanna and Nannu every weekend, and I was thinking that Grandma T must feel left out. I thought I'd go over and see her today after church rather than accompanying you to Aunt Grace's."

"Oh." Mom seemed surprised. "That's a very kind thought, Teresa. You could be right. Grandma T might feel lonely. Maybe we can pick her up and take her to Aunt Grace's for dinner?"

Oops. That wouldn't work. I needed Grandma T to myself.

"No, no. Grandma T and Nannu, they don't really get

along too great. You go visit Nanna and Nannu. They'll be expecting you. And I'll go see Grandma T. I'll tell her you are thinking about her," I added quickly.

"I guess that would work," Mom said slowly. "We'll drop you off after church and pick you up on the way home from Aunt Grace's. And I'll invite Grandma to supper on Wednesday. That was very thoughtful, Teresa." Mom was using positive reinforcement for good behavior.

Oddly, it worked. I felt, well, holy, like a nun who takes a vow of poverty and selflessly helps others. Except, are nuns really selfless? I mean, when you do something kind for someone else, it makes you feel all good inside, which is, in a way, rather selfish. So are nuns being kind to benefit an unfortunate person, or selfishly wanting that good feeling inside? Do you see why it is so hard for me to focus on one thing at a time? All these other thoughts come into my brain without even checking with me first. And what about that vow of chastity? It must certainly make life a lot easier to just take a vow to not have sex. Then you don't have to worry about boys at all. So, who are you taking the vow for? Yourself or God?

And I just had time before church to slip over to see Mrs. Middleton and offer to babysit a couple of evenings next week, which would go a long way to helping solve number two.

n is For NOses, NeRves, AnD NippLes

MSN Message

> T said: 2 good to go for Saturday nite
>
> GLAMGRRL1 said: Grate!

(Obviously, spelling isn't Ashleigh's strong point!)

> GLAMGRRL1 said: Someone special wants to meet you at the party.

Omigawd! It can only be AAA!

> T said: Sure whatever.

Grandma T was quite surprised to see me when Mom dropped me off on the doorstep. In fact, she seemed a bit too surprised, maybe even slightly annoyed. Perhaps she had other plans, like a boyfriend coming over. (Joke. I mean, it's Grandma T, and she's ancient and keeps her teeth in a cup!)

Grandma T lives in the same house where she raised Dad. I looked around at the heavy curtains, the dark furniture, and the uncomfortable chairs with white doily things hung over the backs. Not a book or magazine out of place. I have never been able to imagine Dad as a kid here.

Nor can I imagine Grandma T as a mother. I can't see her putting a Band-Aid on a scraped knee. She'd frown upon any activity that might scrape a knee. Or giving you a kiss before bed. Or reading a story out loud. Maybe Grandpa T did that. Poor Dad. Imagine living all alone in this house. No brothers or sisters. I bet Grandma T locked him in a cupboard in the dark when he was naughty. Very Charles Dickens.

Anyway, I was there and Mom had left, so Grandma T led me into the "sitting room." No standing in this room, I told myself with a little giggle.

I gave a small sniff. Nanna and Nannu's apartment always smells like tomato sauce, basil, or cookies, and you want to breathe deeply. Grandma T's house smells like—I sniffed again, trying to decipher the scents—dead flowers, cleanser, and sour lemons.

"Use a tissue, Teresa," Grandma T said.

"Oh, my nose isn't running. I was just smelling your house," I replied.

Grandma T raised her eyebrows but didn't pursue it.

Right about now I knew Dad was driving around looking for a parking spot with Mom cheering him on, and at Aunt Grace's there would be laughing and ear-splitting shrieks. At Grandma T's, the drawn curtains kept you from laughing loudly. It was going to be a long afternoon, but I was determined to learn England-English from the best, or at least the best I had available to me.

Grandma T and I sat in the sitting room on two wing chairs (I love that name—I always expect them to fly off), facing each other.

"How is school?" she asked. She enunciated every word carefully. She thinks contractions are slang. An English thing, I figured, so I would have to try to copy her.

"Quite decent," I said.

I stared at her mouth, wondering what it is that makes an accent. The way lips form words? Or perhaps it was the shape of a throat or tongue. Maybe all races have their own distinct-shaped tongues. Biff would know. But Biff wasn't speaking to me. Which really was very childish of her. She had obviously forgotten our pact that boyfriends—the having or acquiring of them—takes priority over everything else. And being really smart, she should also have realized that I'm only being friends with the Glams to snare AAA.

"What subjects are you studying?" Grandma T asked.

"English."

And one of those thoughts that fly unbidden into your

mind flew into mine. When you're old like Grandma T, do you still have nipples? I mean, you can't really use them at her age. Like, for feeding babies. Maybe they wither up and drop off and you end up looking like Barbie. And why do guys have nipples? I mean, they never use them either.

Grandma T nodded her head approvingly. "The classics, I hope."

"Uh, yeah. Yes, I mean." Whatever the classics were?

I had to get my mind off nipples. They're definitely not an appropriate thinking subject for a Sunday. Instead, I focused on Grandma T's nose. It is quite large and pointy at the end, with glasses perched halfway down, though I think those are for effect. She always looks over them, never through them. Maybe we *were* descended from royalty. I felt my own nose. Not that big. With changing gene pools and all that stuff, the blue blood might be thinned, but still, it would be there.

Perhaps there was a castle in England that used to be ours, but sadly fell into the bad duke's hands. I could moan about that to AAA (in my England-English). Maybe he'd say something like, "I will get your castle back for you, milady." (I know, I know. Empowered woman. I should fight for my own castle. Blah, blah, blah. But the truth is, I want to be helpless, and AAA, well, I want him to be helpful.) And there would be a sword fight on a high stone turret between AAA and the bad duke, and AAA would be killed, and I'd never marry out of loyalty to him. Instead

I'd walk the castle halls, become their resident ghost, and mourn my love forever.

"Is literature all you study?"

I started. My romantic non-feminist dream shattered into tiny pieces of castle stone. "Math, gym, and health." I grimaced, thinking of running laps around the sweaty gym.

"Do not pull your face into such expressions, Teresa," Grandma T said. "It is most unbecoming."

"Sorry," I muttered.

"And sit up straight like a young lady. You will get bad nerves if you slump."

I had no idea you could get bad nerves from slumping. Maybe your nerves go all the way through your back from your butt to your brain and if your spine isn't straight, the nerves get all tangled up before they hit the brain and thus are "bad" nerves.

"Your father had bad nerves as a child, though heaven knows why. I made him sit straight."

I sat up and glanced around the dismal sitting room. I wish I'd gone to Aunt Grace's house instead. No one there cared if I slumped. And Nannu P would grab me and we would dance around the room and my spine would straighten and my nerves wouldn't go bad.

"And History," I finished. "I have to do a project on World War II."

"I was eight years old during the London Blitz," Grandma T said.

"You were there?" I was surprised.

"Yes. The bombing was dreadful. Finally, after one near miss, my mother sent me away to the country to keep me safe. We were child evacuees. I did not want to go. I did not want to leave my mother. But you did what you were told in those days," she added sternly.

"Where did you stay?" I asked, interested despite myself.

"With a farm family. I think they mostly wanted someone to help with the chores and to take care of their babies. But I suppose it was better than the bombs. London was burning. I stayed with that family for three years." She smiled. "I was not so badly off. I was fed well, lots of milk and fresh apples and vegetables. There was very little food in London. But I missed my mother dreadfully. My father was overseas, so it was just she and I."

An idea began to take hold. Grandma T and Nannu could be my History project! They had both been kids during World War II. They were living history. But first things first, as Grandma T would say.

I pulled out a notebook and pen. "Grandma, I'm also doing a project on the English language. That's England-English," I explained. "What are some English words?"

"I am afraid I do not quite follow you. Do you mean words that we use for an item that are different from your word for the same item?"

I nodded. That would do.

"Well, for example, we use the word 'lift,' whereas you use the word 'elevator.'"

I scribbled that down.

"And you say 'apartment' and we say 'flat.'"

She continued through a list of words while I scribbled them down. Finally she ran out. We sat for a while.

"Would you like some tea?"

Now, what could be more English than tea?

"That would be very nice," I said primly. A very English response. I'm a fast learner. Maybe it had something to do with sitting up straight.

I followed Grandma into the kitchen and set out four "biscuits" (England-English for cookies) while Grandma boiled water and made tea.

"Did you ever want to go back to live in England?" I asked Grandma T.

"Good heavens no," she said. "It's far too drafty."

Windy England.

She placed two china cups and saucers (no mugs here) on a tray, along with milk and sugar, and carried it into the sitting room. I followed with the biscuits. Now this was *very* English. Tea in china cups with store-bought biscuits, while sitting in wing chairs, and it was even November—rainy and cold outside. And inside. I was freezing. I wish she'd turn up the heat.

"Do you want me to put on the fire?" Grandma T must have seen me shiver.

"A fire would be nice," I replied.

Grandma T walked over to the fireplace and pushed

a button. Fake flames leapt up, while an electric heater pumped out warm air. I guess that is what they call a "fire" in England.

I dumped three teaspoons of sugar into my cup and filled it half full of milk. Grandma T raised her eyebrows but said nothing, merely filled the remaining half of my cup with tea. I sipped daintily, and then it suddenly hit me. The cup in my hand was like the china cup Grandma T put her teeth into! OMIGAWD!

I spluttered tea everywhere in an attempt to spit it back into the cup, and set it back on the saucer with a sharp *clink*.

"What on earth is the matter?" Grandma T asked. Alarmed, she looked into her own cup.

"It was too sweet," I said.

I grabbed my napkin and wiped my lips (and tongue) and down the front of my sweater where the tea had dribbled.

"Would you care for another cup? Perhaps with less sugar?"

"No, I'm fine." I peeked at my watch. Another hour until Mom and Dad came. I needed a survival plan.

Grandma glanced at her own wrist.

"There is a good mystery show on television on Sunday afternoons at three," Grandma T said.

So *that* was why she was annoyed when I arrived—a favorite television show ruined.

"That sounds good." More research.

I grabbed my pencil and notebook, and held them ready. Grandma T switched on the television.

Ten minutes later, my pen was still poised over the blank paper. Truth was, I couldn't understand a word anyone said. I did note, though, that English women laugh like horses whinnying. I'd have to practice that at home.

An hour later, show over, I had added only three words to my list: "smashing" and "snogging" and "shagging." The first word meant "great!" "Snogging" meant "kissing," and "shagging" meant, well, "doing it." Yes, *that* IT. Grandma sniffed when she heard that word, but her disapproval wasn't strong enough to make her turn the show off.

English is a weird language. "Snogging" sounds like something you would do in a pond with your jeans rolled up to your knees, and "shagging" keeps reminding me of carpet, or sheep dogs. Not particularly *seksi* (Maltese for sexy). So, in my multilingual mode, I would say that AAA is both "smashing" and "*seksi*."

When Mom and Dad finally picked me up, I gave Grandma a demure (Victorian word) hug goodbye. Surprisingly, she pecked me on the cheek and said, "Goodbye, dear."

Then she told Mom and Dad that my visit had been most enjoyable and that she'd recounted her childhood days to me. She said I was turning into a lovely young lady. I guess she forgot about the teacup spitting incident. Thank goodness old people are forgetful.

As we got near the car, I grabbed Dad in a huge hug.

"I'm really sorry about your nose and the castle and the dark cupboard and not having Band-Aids and no one to read a book to you. And if you stood up straight, you'd have better nerves."

Dad's eyes widened and his eyebrows went up almost to his hairline.

"Oh, and don't make your face all weird like that, Dad. It's unbecoming."

He and Mom exchanged a puzzled glance.

"Well, come on, then," I said. "Let's get home."

As soon as I got into the house, I checked the telephone for messages. Not that I was expecting anything from her, but there was nothing from Biff. I logged onto the computer to look at my e-mail. Again, not because I was expecting anything from Biff, because I wasn't, but if there *was* a message from her, I'd probably look at it. There was nothing from Biff. There was, though, something from Phillip.

E-mail
5:00 p.m.
To: T
From: PHILMAN
Subject: R U OK?

> You and Biff should talk. She told me today that she misses you.
>
> Phil

Biff was talking about *me* to Phil! That is in total violation of the best friend code.

"It's like breaking a commandment," I told Barbie. "Thou shalt not discuss thy best friend with outsiders!" How could Elizabeth (I refuse to call her Biff anymore) do that to me?

15

O is For Opportunity

They say that when opportunity knocks, you should open the door. Well, I'm opening it wide and inviting opportunity (a.k.a. AAA) in with open arms.

Now that I was even closer to being AAA's girlfriend, it was imperative that I have my own bathroom. I anticipated many hours of preparations to look good for MY BOYFRIEND. I knew exactly the look I wanted. A *snog*-me look, but not a *shag*-me look. And there's a very fine line between the two—a line that a girl does not want to cross. Otherwise, she's a skank. So it was going to take a lot of work, work I could not be doing with Hugo banging on the bathroom door.

I poured a glass of orange juice. I hate Monday mornings.

Note to School Administrators: A good time to start school is 10:00 a.m., not 8:20.

The average teenager is not coherent before 10:00 a.m. and even that is pushing it.

Dad was filling his travel mug with coffee from the pot. Mom turned a page of the newspaper.

Note to Teenagers Who Want Something from Parents: Soften them up first with compliments. Even old people like parents like to be flattered.

"You're looking pretty good these days, Dad," I said. He was my target today. After all, he was the one in the construction industry.

He glanced down at his steel-toed boots and paint-stained khaki pants.

"Oh yeah, just a little thing, Dad," I continued. "Could you make Sophia's bedroom into a bathroom for me? After she's gone, of course," I added. A little mature jocularity to show I'm an adult who can wait until her sister moves out. Unless Sophia should happen to move out earlier, maybe even by this weekend? In fact, in this day and age, why wasn't she already living with Anthony?

"A bathroom?" Coffee spilled over the top of his cup onto his hand. I won't repeat his next word. Not fit for tender ears.

"Yeah. I thought you could knock out the wall between Sophia's room and mine and make it an ensuite."

Mom looked at me as if I had sprouted a second head. I felt my shoulder. Nope, only one.

"That's going to be the baby's room," Mom said.

"I thought Boo-Boo would sleep with you," I said. "Isn't that supposed to be, like, a bonding experience or something, for the baby to sleep with the parents? I'm sure I saw that on television, though it was about chimpanzees. But since we're descended from apes I thought the same rules should apply. I really need my own bathroom." My adult maturity quickly regressed into whiny kid.

Suddenly, Boo-Boo's arrival seemed very real. She was costing me a bathroom! Already I was experiencing middle-child trauma.

"Don't worry your mother," Dad yelled at me.

"Marshall," Mom began, "perhaps Teresa is experiencing feelings of displacement with the arrival of... "

"She's a spoiled brat," Dad interrupted. "*I need my own bathroom.*" He mimicked me! My exact whine!

Note to Parents: If you want to irreparably harm your children—mimic them.

Why was Dad doing all the yelling? Something was definitely not right here. Sophia, Hugo, and I knew that Mom was the disciplinarian in this house. That's when I noticed the dark half-moons underneath her eyes.

I blurted out the first thought in my head. "You're not going to die, are you, Mom?"

Note to the Unwary: Do not blurt out the first thought that comes into your head. It's generally not a good one. Wait until the second thought, then blurt that one out.

"What on earth makes you think—"

"What kind of stupid question is that?" Dad interrupted Mom—again.

I waited for her to tell him that we don't use the word "stupid" in our house. But she didn't. Obviously, that only applies to kids!

"Marshall, didn't you have a meeting at eight?" Mom asked.

Dad grabbed his jacket from the back of the chair. "No more upsetting your mother. She's got enough to think about. And clean up the breakfast dishes before school. You should help out more around here. A bathroom!" He glared at me and left.

Tears pricked behind my eyes. Dad had yelled at me. He never yelled at me. I was the baby of the family. But obviously not anymore; Boo-Boo had pushed me out.

Mom said, "Dad's just worried because I didn't sleep too well last night. I'm perfectly fine. But I'm going to take today off work and rest a bit." She reached out and pulled me to her side. "I'm certainly not going to die. Or at least, not for a long time. Don't worry."

But *she* was worried about something. I could tell.

Walking to school fifteen minutes later, a scrap of conversation I'd overheard Mom and Dad have in the car on the way home from Grandma T's returned to me.

I'd been in the back seat practicing my England-English words: *snogging, lift, flat, shagging.* Mom said something about Nannu and his memory. Dad told her all old people become forgetful with age, but Mom thought it was something more. Dad said it was just the baby making her nervous and more sensitive than usual. (Which is funny, because Grandma T says Dad is the one who has bad nerves.) Was Nannu sick?

I arrived at the corner of Jones and Hincks streets, but there was no one there. Fine, if Elizabeth didn't want to walk with me, I could walk by myself. I mean, there is absolutely nothing wrong with walking alone to school. I was a confident girl who enjoyed her own company. I didn't *need* anyone to walk to school with me. *I* had an almost-boyfriend

Fantasy: Spine straight, I march right into school, head high, dispensing generous smiles right and left because I am now an AN.
Reality: I slouch in behind a group of kids with my head down and hope no one notices me on my own because they might think I'm an SN.

I got out my books for morning classes, banged my locker shut, took a deep breath, and sidled up to Big Bertha. She was pulling gym clothes from her locker and tossing them into a backpack. Five dollars in my fist, I tapped her shoulder.

"Uh, thanks, Bertha, I'm sorry I didn't get this back

to you sooner. I had to babysit to get the money," I muttered out of the side of my mouth. You'd think it was a drug deal. Suddenly, I remembered the school surveillance cameras. Would they think it *was* a drug deal? I could be in jail by nightfall and miss the party Saturday. I put on a big smile. See? No drug deal here. Drug dealers don't smile.

She did up the straps on her bag, not taking the money, forcing me to stand there. Finally she straightened up. "That's not my name," she said.

"What?"

"Big Bertha is what the kids here call me, but my name is Talia." She glowered at me.

I was surprised. "Talia. That's a really pretty name."

"Are you saying it's too pretty for me?"

She thrust her face into mine and I stepped back. She could beat me to a pulp with one smack of her giant hand.

"No, I'm saying that's a really pretty name." And I meant it. "I'm named after a saint," I added.

"A saint?" Talia laughed.

I shrugged. "Yeah, well, you know. It was my mom's idea. Ever the optimist."

Ber … Talia almost smiled. She had great eyes. A shade of blue that verged on purple and long, black lashes framing them.

"Anyway, thanks a lot," I said. I thrust the money into her hand and walked quickly to homeroom. It wouldn't do to be seen talking to an SN for too long.

Making my way to my desk, I suddenly saw Elizabeth on the other side of the room, talking to some kids and pretending not to see me. So I pretended not to see her. No way was I seeing her first. If she noticed me, and wanted to talk to me, that was fine. I'd be happy to talk to her. But I wasn't making the first move. I hadn't done anything wrong. But for some reason my conscience pricked, nope, *stabbed* me!

Then I saw Elizabeth sit down. WAY OVER ON THE OTHER SIDE OF THE ROOM. She'd switched seats to get away from me. Well, if that was the way she wanted it. She should use herself for an anthropology study! How childish to change seats. It was obvious who was the more mature person here. (Me, in case it's not that obvious.)

Apparently she didn't understand the concept of opportunity knocking at the door. Didn't she realize that I had to open the door of opportunity to let AAA in or forever lose the chance to have him for a boyfriend? Even in school they teach us to take advantage of every opportunity that comes our way. True, they probably mean for schoolwork or jobs or character-building stuff, but I think the same philosophy could apply to getting a boyfriend.

As I slowly lowered myself into my chair, tears stung my eyes.

Ashleigh leaned over from her seat. "Saturday's party is going to be so great. And like I said, someone special wants to meet you," she added coyly. (Normally I would hate that singsong tone of voice, but as it applied to AAA, I found I could easily forgive her.)

My heart lurched. I gasped for air. This being-in-love business was seriously affecting my health.

Phillip came rushing in and screeched to a halt at my desk. "Where were you this morning? We waited for you, but it got late so we left," he said.

So Elizabeth had waited for me? I stole a glance over at her. She probably thought *I'd* not wanted to walk with *her*. This was getting too complicated for me.

"We're talking here," Ashleigh said pointedly.

"Uh, yeah, we're talking," I muttered to Phillip.

He glanced at Ashleigh, then back at me. "Okay. Maybe I'll see you after school."

He strode down the aisle to his desk.

"So, is your brother coming Saturday?" Ashleigh asked.

"Yep," I said. He'd be there if I had to tie him up and drag him to that party. No one was going to spoil this opportunity for me. Not Hugo, not Elizabeth, not anyone. The man of my dreams would soon be my boyfriend.

I sat through announcements, gasping for breath and trying not to throw up. Don't you *love* being in love?

p is For pARty AnD pARents

(warning: do not mix together, highly combustible)

My eyes flew open. Saturday morning. Party day. My stomach churned. It had been a confusing week. Between party planning, trying to keep up with the Glams' demands (it's expensive being part of their group), plus the energy expended avoiding Elizabeth, I was exhausted. I'd even babysat D and D twice this week. With all that going on, I also had to do school work!

Having said that, my party prep list was in good shape, as were my butt cheeks from the daily bum crunches I was doing. I had my England-English words down pat (smashing!) and I'd practiced clever things to say to AAA, but not too clever.

Advice to Females: Do not appear smarter than your date. Guys' egos are very fragile.

Yesterday after school, Ashleigh, Kara, and I had made a quick trip to the mall to buy me an incredible new top, with an incredible price that left nothing for a new bra. I'd have to make do with the old one and a sock.

After shopping, Ashleigh suggested we go back to MY house to hang out. My hands immediately turned clammy. The Glams! In my house! OMIGAWD! They'd see where I lived! They would meet my family! And Dad, he'd just stand there saying nothing, which can be a bit creepy if you don't know him. I said I'd have to ask Mom and I just hoped like crazy she'd say no. I pretended to look for my pretend cell phone in my purse until Kara lent me hers. And wouldn't you know, for once Mom was cooperative and said it was fine to have my friends over. She just had to be great, when I wanted her *not* to be. Honestly, parents!

At my house, Ashleigh spent the entire time talking about Hugo (a crashing bore—England-English) and going into the hall from my bedroom hoping to accidentally-on-purpose bump into Hugo.

There were really only two Embarrassing Moments (EMs):

EM No. 1: Kara picked up my Barbie and Ken from the bed and said, "You don't actually play with these anymore, do you?"

I snatched the dolls from her and said, "I have no idea how they got here. Mom must have been tidying up."

I tossed them into the bottom of the closet with as much disdain as I could muster, while silently apologizing. Barbie has really been there for me when I needed her.

EM No. 2: Nanna and Nannu just happened to be passing by and dropped in. Yeah, right. Thanks for embarrassing me, Mom. At least Nanna brought cookies.

After the Glams left, Nannu told me he didn't think Ashleigh was a good friend for me. "She too nice, that girl," he said. I know that doesn't sound like a horrible thing, but I knew what he meant. Ashleigh was overly sweet to Nanna and Nannu, sucking up.

"Where's that Buff girl?" Nannu asked me. Not once, but about five times. "I like that girl." Also repeated five times.

Mind you, Ashleigh wasn't overly sweet when she left. Hugo never came home and on the way out she growled, "You better be sure he comes to the party."

Hoping to discover Hugo's appeal to the fairer sex, I took a good look at him at breakfast while he attacked a bowl of cereal. Milk dribbled down his chin, his hair stood on end, one cheek had red creases from his pillow and he smelled of BO. Seriously. What does Ashleigh see in him?

After lunch, in an effort to suck up to Sophia, who owns the only straightening iron in the house—do you know how much those things cost?—I helped tie ribbons around little scented sachets for favors for the wedding shower that I was giving Sophia. Well, I was giving it in name only. In reality, Sophia was giving her own shower. She'd picked the theme and color scheme, designed the invitations and chosen the guests, food, and favors. I bet she'd even given her guests a list of presents to bring.

Feeling generous, I even felt Mom's stomach when the baby kicked.

What I said: That's so cool. She kicked me.

Which delighted Mom because she thought it meant I was finally accepting Boo-Boo. Hey, I have no problem with the impending birth, I just had lots of other things on my mind.

What I really thought: Eeewww. Is it just me or is the thought of having another living being inside you sort of gross? It's like a science fiction story. I mean, what if it's really an alien baby? And how do all the mother's guts not get squished? Yuck. Thinking about that makes me feel queasy. I'm not sure I'm cut out to be a mother. Maybe AAA and I will adopt. Or perhaps we'll just have pets.

At two o'clock, I decided it was time to start the Preparations. I pushed my chair back from the table.

"Where do you think you're going?" Sophia demanded. "We're not done here yet."

"I have to get ready for the school-spirit party," I said.

"Yeah, *school-spirit* party." Sophia snorted her disbelief.

"That is really quite an unattractive habit you have," I said primly. "What does Anthony think of it?"

I swear I heard Mom snicker, but all she said was, "Girls." Then, "Let her go get ready, Sophia. We can finish up here."

"I'm going to need the bathroom for the next four hours," I said. "Does anyone want to use it before me?" See, I'm progressing quite nicely in the maturity area, by being generous with my bathroom time.

"Four hours!" Sophia shrieked. "To get ready for a pep rally?"

"A school-spirit party," I said. "And can I borrow some of your bubble bath?"

Sophia squinted at me for a moment. "Yeah, go ahead, party girl. And I'll straighten your hair for you when you're done."

I couldn't believe that she'd actually offered before I even asked. That was so un-Sophia-like.

"Thanks," I said.

"If you're going out you should look decent. I used to go to that school, you know. We have a reputation to keep up."

Party Preparation Time for Girls: four hours.
Party Preparation Time for Boys: ten minutes

We girls spend way too much time trying to make ourselves gorgeous for guys, who, in return, put no effort into their appearance. Hugo pulled on a clean T-shirt, splashed on after-shave (though he didn't shave!), and was ready to go. Actually, I was glad he was going. I didn't want to arrive on my own.

I turned around in front of Mom's full-length mirror, admiring myself. I looked pretty hot, if I did say so myself. I loved my straight hair. It had taken Sophia almost an hour of bitching, but she'd done a great job.

"Here." Sophia came in with an eye-glitter stick. "This will sparkle you up." She applied the makeup to my eyelids. "Keep your drink with you at all times."

"Drink? It's a school party," I said innocently.

"Hey, even Mom knows you're not going to a *pep rally*."

"She does?"

"Yeah. She's not stupid," Sophia said. "Besides, you're just about jumping out of your skin with first-major-party nerves."

She spread gloss over my lips.

"Anyway, don't drink too much because you're not used to alcohol. Pour it yourself and don't ever leave your drink alone. Keep it with you."

"Why?" I asked.

"Some people are total scum. They put drugs into other people's drinks."

"Oh," I said. I didn't realize parties could be dangerous.

As we left the house, Mom asked, "Are the parents going to be there?"

"Of course," I said. I really had no idea. In fact, I had no idea who was having the party. Hugo knew that and told Dad where to go.

As we left the car, Dad said to Hugo, "You take care of your sister."

"Sure thing," Hugo said.

"Right, then. I'll pick you up at eleven thirty." Dad squinted at the lit-up house, reluctant to leave.

Cars lined the street, and more were parked on the lawn. Music blasted. "Pretty big party, by the looks of it. Are you sure the parents are home?"

"Yep. Do you want to come in to meet them?" Hugo asked.

I hate to admit it, but Hugo was brilliant. (This one time, anyway.)

"That's okay," Dad said quickly. "Eleven thirty. Be out here." He drove away.

"Excellent move," I said. "Like Dad would ever want to meet the parents."

Hugo grinned. "Like there'd be any parents here to meet!"

No parents? That made my stomach lurch. I think I actually thought parents would be there.

"Whose house is this?" I asked.

"Greg's."

"He's a moron," I said. I was stalling. I was suddenly

terrified of going in. I didn't know how to behave at parties. What if no one talked to me? If Biff—no, Elizabeth—was here, she would talk to me. I couldn't believe I'm going to my first high school party without my best friend who was no longer my best friend.

"I'll pretend I don't know you if you pretend you don't know me," Hugo said.

"Deal," I agreed.

I mean, who arrives at a party with their sister or brother?

I squeezed my way inside between two burly guys with beers in their fists. They were talking to two girls whose skirts barely covered their backsides. Grandma T would have been sniffing her disapproval non-stop if she'd seen that!

The place was packed, and I didn't recognize a single person. Omigawd! I was going to be the token wallflower! The confidence of an entire week of preparation quickly fizzled away. I looked awful. I had a sock stuffed in my bra! And why had I straightened my hair? And jeans? What was I thinking? Every girl here was wearing a skirt.

Thump! Thump! The loud bass tingled through my feet to my head, making me dizzy. A kissing couple blocked the doorway, and when I'd finally pried them apart so I could leave, two kids came through the door and swept me back into the room, and suddenly I was at the party whether I liked it or not.

Wall-to-wall kids. I stealthily inched my way along the living room wall to a dining room. Maybe there was a back door. Guys were filling glasses from a keg—OMIGAWD! Alcohol! Everyone had a glass of booze. I was at a party with alcohol! Be cool, I told myself. *Pretend you always come to parties where there is alcohol.* I tried to look bored as I continued to inch my way along the wall.

A hand reached out and grabbed my upper arm. I jumped a mile.

"There you are," Ashleigh said. "You look like a deer caught in the headlights. Relax." She had a glass of beer in her hand. Foam slopped over the side of the glass and spilled on the carpet as she dragged me through to the kitchen. "Where's Hugo?" she yelled over the music.

"He's here somewhere," I shouted back.

"Okay, I'll find him in a moment. Now, someone is dying to meet you. Close your eyes," she ordered.

Note to the Unwary: Never close your eyes when someone tells you to. Peek from beneath your lashes. It will save you a lot of grief later.

I never got a chance to close my eyes because Ashleigh suddenly spun me around. And there were Greg and AAA leaning against the kitchen counter, a half-eaten bag of potato chips between them.

First Thought: I'm going to faint.
Second Thought: No, I'm not.
Third Thought: Yes, I am.

Fourth Thought: Brain, don't you dare embarrass me! Say something clever—RIGHT NOW!

"Bonjour," I said.

Adam laughed. "See?" He poked Greg. "Multilingual. I told you she was cute."

That was the best moment in my entire life so far.

"This is a *smashing* party," I said in my best Grandma T voice. I tried an English whinnying laugh. They all stared at me. Okay, I won't do that again.

"Teresa, this is Greg," Ashleigh said. "The someone I've been telling you about who wants to meet you."

"You mean Adam," I said.

"No, Greg."

Greg? Greg wanted to meet me? Neanderthal Greg?

That was the worst moment in my entire life so far.

"Oh," I said. No accent this time. "I get you two mixed up sometimes because you're always together," I finished weakly.

Adam clapped Greg on the shoulder. "See you around." He winked at me and I was alone with Greg; or as alone as you can be, surrounded by a roomful of people.

"So, do you want a beer?" Greg asked.

I shook my head.

"Something else?"

"Um...wine?" I said. Nannu had given me sips of wine before.

"I think Dad has some of that around here." Greg

pushed his way through the crowd to a wine cabinet built beneath a cupboard.

This was it. The moment to make my escape while Greg wasn't looking. But my feet were rooted to the floor, and he was back with a glass of white wine and the moment was gone.

"So, this is your house?" I asked. I had to yell to be heard over the music and voices.

"Yup. My parents are down south," he yelled back. "They'll be home tomorrow sometime."

"They don't mind you having a party?"

He laughed. "They don't know."

I took a gulp of the wine. My cheeks sucked in, it was so sour. I suddenly remembered Sophia's warning about drinks. Was something in it? I should have poured it myself. Or maybe wine was always this yucky.

"So, what languages do you speak?" he asked.

"A little Maltese, Australian, and English-English, like from England," I said.

"And French," Greg added.

"Huh?"

"You said, *Bonjoor.*"

"Oh yeah, a little French." Very little.

"I thought maybe you were going out with that other guy," Greg said. "The dork that always seems to be around you."

"Phillip?" See, I told Elizabeth we'd be tainted by him always hanging around. She never listens to me.

I forced a laugh—but didn't go for a whinny this time. "Oh, *puhleeze*. He sort of tags along behind us. Like a stray puppy. We used to be friends years and years ago, and I guess he still thinks we are. I feel sort of sorry for him." I downed my glass of wine, hoping to shut off my conscience which was smacking me hard.

Greg poured me another glass. I downed that one, too. My conscience was really bugging me.

"You feel sorry for Maggot? You're too soft-hearted," Greg said. "Besides, he's just asking to have his ass kicked with that briefcase."

Funny, I'd had a very similar thought. Maybe Greg wasn't so awful. In fact, he looked sort of cute at the moment. And he was on the football team. He drained his beer, crushed the can with his hand, and tossed it into the sink. He immediately grabbed another.

"That blonde chick you hang around with, she's hot."

Guys Listen Up: No girl likes to hear about another girl who's hot! Especially when that first girl just spent hours trying to make herself look hot!

"Yeah, I guess she's okay-looking," I said, somewhat miffed. I mean, hey, I'm standing right here with my hair straightened. I couldn't look any hotter.

"If she'd lose the glasses, that is," Greg went on.

"I'm always telling her that," I said.

Greg and I actually thought quite a bit alike. I was warming up to him.

"Well, my man over there," Greg gestured with his beer can toward Adam, "would appreciate getting to know her a little better. Maybe you could tell her that. We could all go out together sometime."

If Greg had slapped me, I couldn't have been more shocked. Adam liked Elizabeth! Elizabeth! All this time I'd thought she was helping me get AAA to notice me, and it turned out she was helping herself—to my boyfriend!

"More wine?" Greg asked.

I was surprised to see my glass empty. "Yeah," I said.

Now I was drowning my hurt. Adam liked my ex-best friend.

Greg refilled my glass and we talked a bit. Another refill. He put his arm around my shoulders and we went through to the family room. The lights were turned low. Couples danced close together. Others sprawled on the sofa, limbs entangled, tongues cleaning each other's tonsils. And then it hit me. I, Teresa Tolliver, was at a great party.

Now, I know it was AAA that I wanted as a boyfriend, but it felt pretty cool to have Greg's arm around me. That arm got me into the "inner circle." That arm gave me immediate status and all the AN perks that went along with that.

We pushed into a group that included Hugo. Ashleigh was at his elbow, frantically swinging her blonde hair, hoping he'd notice her. He didn't. If she kept that up, her head might just swivel off her body. I started to laugh and couldn't stop.

"What's so funny?" Greg asked.

"Ashleigh. Head coming off," I gasped.

Hugo noticed me. "Hey," he said to Greg, "don't give her drinks. She can't handle it."

"Oh, stop wining." I whooped with laughter. "Get it? Wining? Whining?" Had I ever been funnier?

Suddenly the overhead lights came on and the music stopped. Dead silence. Couples untangled, blinked at the brightness, and clothes were quickly straightened.

"What the hell's going on here?" A man's voice demanded.

"Oh crap," Greg said.

His parents.

q is For QuAntity theoRy

Quantum Theory: The theory that energy can only be absorbed or radiated in discrete values or quanta.

I have no idea what this means either. Physics is next term.
    I do know what my Quantity Theory means.

Quantity Theory: When there is too much going on in your brain (that's the quantity part) and it explodes. Your brain, not the theory.

Examples: The Elizabeth and me situation.
    The Greg and me situation.
    The Adam and me situation.
    The Adam and Elizabeth situation.
    The toilet and me situation. (Too much wine—spent

the night heaving. Told Mom I had the flu. Don't think she believed me, but she wiped my face anyway as I lay on the bathroom floor, and told me that it was a learning experience I was, well, experiencing. Psychology 101.)

E-mail
10:10 a.m.
To: T
From: GLAMGRRL1
Subject: Debt

> You owe me! I got Greg for you. Now you have to get Hugo for me or else!

" ... Except," I complained to Barbie, "it's not Greg I want. It's Adam."

I was in bed. Mom was letting me stay home from church, though Dad said it would probably do me some good to go.

"And have her being sick in church?" Mom said.

Dad said Hugo had to go, then, because he was supposed to be looking out for me. Notice Dad never said *he* was going. Mom said he should have gone in and met the parents before leaving us there, and that he was going to have to get over his phobia sometime. It was a very un-Sunday-like argument.

Despite the messy aftermath, I must admit it was a great party. While it lasted. You never saw people leave a house so fast, though threats involving police do tend to speed up exiting times. Hugo borrowed a cell phone (see?

I should have one in case of emergency, like being kicked out of a party) and called Dad to pick us up.

"Act normal," he said to me while we waited for Dad. "But not too normal. That's a dead giveaway that you've been drinking, because you're not that normal, normally. And chew this." He pushed a stick of gum into my hand. "You stink. And try not to breathe in front of Dad."

"All human *beingsh haffta* breathe," I told Hugo with a giggle.

"Breathe through your nose then, you idiot, and stop laughing. And don't say anything! You're slurring your words."

I made it fine through the car ride, and Hugo hustled me past Mom, who'd sat up "to be there for me" if I wanted to discuss my first teenage party—which I didn't, though I felt bad when I saw her disappointment. Head spinning, I made it to my room. An hour later was when the—to put it bluntly—puking began. That's when I did need Mom "to be there for me."

My stomach was sore today but I felt better, so I was going over the party details with Barbie and Ken, once again resurrected from my closet.

"And now I don't even know if I'm Greg's girlfriend or not," I finished.

Ken said that he thought *he* was my boyfriend.

"Oh, stop your *wining*," I told him. "*Whining*, get it?" I still thought that was the funniest joke ever, even though it made me feel a bit nauseous to remember it. "Anyway, you're a doll. And besides, Barbie is your girlfriend."

Ken assured us he could handle two girls at once.

Barbie and I shook our heads. Guys!

"And isn't there a law against sending threatening e-mails?" I said. "That Ashleigh is lucky I'm not calling the police." While Dad was in the basement for a few minutes checking hammers or saws or something, I had tiptoed down and checked my e-mail. I wished I hadn't.

Barbie said I should probably call a lawyer.

"Yeah, and one to sue Elizabeth too. Can you believe her going after Adam when she knew I liked him?"

Barbie agreed I was in quite a quandary. In fact there were a lot of "Q" words that applied to my situation right now.

Quandary: I wanted AAA, but it was Greg I got.
Quarrel: with Elizabeth.

A tear ran down Barbie's perfect doll face.

"It's okay," I told her as I sniffled. "You don't have to cry."

Oh, oh, another "Q" word.

Queasy: I made a run for the bathroom.

Mom did make me go to Sunday dinner at Aunt Grace's, despite my head pounding (a flu-bug, I said; a hangover, Sophia announced) and a tongue that felt like it was covered in that furry gunk you get on old food from the back of the fridge. Anthony kept shoving pasta in front of my face just to watch me wince. Maybe he deserves Sophia after all!

I was sitting at the dinner table, picking away at a slice of bread, the only thing I could even think about eating, when Nannu poked me.

"So, that boy. The one you like. Was he at the party?"

That was a signal for all my uncles to tease me about boyfriends, and my Aunt Grace to tell my mother I was too young to be out at parties. Funny how Nannu could remember that, but he couldn't recollect Anthony's name, which really made Sophia mad. Life might throw crap at you, but there's always a silver lining.

I did get a chance to ask Nannu if he'd help me with my History project. My idea was that I would invite Grandma T and Nannu to come and speak to my class about World War II from a living-history point of view. I'd asked Mr. Timber and he had agreed, saying it was an original, innovative idea. More importantly for me, Nannu and Grandma T would do my project and I'd get the credit.

"That's a wonderful idea," Mom said. She threw a triumphant glance at Aunt Grace. *See?* it said. *She's a smart girl.* "You'll enjoy doing that, won't you, Pa? You'll like meeting all those young people. It's a great idea," she repeated.

Nannu was quite excited. "Except, we don't need that old English woman," he said.

"Pa! That's Marshall's mother you're talking about."

Mom looked pointedly at Dad, but it went right over Nannu's head.

He was busy thinking about the project. In the middle of dessert, he pushed away from the table and grabbed his coat. "I have slides at home of the limestone caves we stayed in when they bombed Malta. I go find them." He left, banging the door behind him.

"Pa," Mom and her sisters called, but his car backed out of the driveway and he was gone, without Nanna.

As we drove her home later that afternoon, Nanna thanked me for my idea as it would get him out from under her "chin" (I think she meant "feet") for a while. "All day, all he does is watch his weather," Nanna said.

"This will give him an interest," Mom said.

Arriving home, I phoned Grandma T (despite Nannu's objections), who agreed to take part.

"It will be very instructional for the students to have a first-hand account of war, which will help them to understand the impact of hostilities and ... "

There was more, but I sort of tuned out after that.

See? Not only was I going to get a great History mark for little effort, but I was helping the elderly, too. I should also get my credit for community service.

A little later that evening, Mom and Dad came into my bedroom, TOGETHER! AND SHUT THE DOOR BEHIND THEM!

Note to the Unwary: United parents and shut doors mean trouble!

I decided to head them off before they could start.

"Okay, I drank just one glass of wine at the party. Well, it might have been two," I babbled. "Three at the most."

"You stunk like a winery," Dad began.

"We'll discuss that in a few minutes," Mom interrupted. "But first, your father and I *want to talk to you.*"

Translation: I want to talk to you and I made Dad come, too.

Mom and Dad sat on the edge of my bed.

"About boys," Mom was saying. "Hugo said you were friendly with one boy in particular at the party. Dad and I feel that you are a bit young to be dating..."

Hugo was a jerk, ratting me out like that.

"I'll be fifteen next month," I said.

"But we feel you *are* mature enough to handle a boy-friend."

Well, I hadn't expected that! Hey, I get to date!

"We *do* want to meet the young man when he comes to take you out," Mom continued.

Omigawd! They sounded like Victorian parents. Next they'd send Nanna to chaperone me on our dates!

"We also want to know where you are going, who you are with, and ask that you respect your curfew of eleven thirty. And no dating on school nights."

"You want me fresh for school," I muttered.

"Exactly," Mom agreed.

Mom must have memorized the entire Parent Your Teen course.

"We want you to know that you can call us at any time if you need us. We don't ever want you getting into a car with this boy, or anyone for that matter, if he or she has been drinking. We won't be mad. We'll just be happy that you were responsible enough to call us."

"Okay," I agreed. This wasn't so bad.

"Now, we know with Sophia's wedding and the new baby that you might have been feeling a little ignored lately. And sometimes girls seek boys' attention to make up for lack of it at home."

Huh? Where was she going with this? Dad was looking increasingly uncomfortable.

"Teenagers have a lot of hormones raging in their bodies, lots of different sensations and urges ... "

OMIGAWD! Sex. She was talking about sex. In front of Dad. I pushed Barbie and Ken farther under the blankets. No need for them to witness my humiliation.

"But your brain hasn't caught up to those sensations yet, and while your body might feel mature enough, your ability to make good decisions is not. Teen pregnancy is on the rise ... "

OMIDOUBLEGAWD! I'd been to exactly one party and she already had me having a baby. I didn't even know if I had a real boyfriend or not!

Dad's face was crimson, and sweat ran down the sides of his cheeks.

"Remember, it is your body for you to do with as you want. You need to treat it with respect. You are a beautiful girl and boys are going to want to do ... um ... things, but you don't have to let anyone do anything to you that makes you uncomfortable. And if you feel you can't handle it, if you feel you're being pressured in any way, I want you to know you can come to me or Dad ... "

I handed Dad a tissue to mop his forehead.

" ... and tell us. It's true we have been busy lately, and we're sorry. We'll try to spend more time with you."

"Really, Mom, I don't feel ignored," I quickly interrupted.

I already spent every Sunday afternoon with my family. I could do with a little more *inattention*.

"And remember we love you very much."

Dad gasped for air.

"Now, is there anything you want to talk to us about?" Mom asked.

"Umm ... nope. Everything's good." Except it was a tie to see who would die of embarrassment first, me or Dad.

"Now about the drinking ... "

Distraction Time: All teens should know the art of distraction. It's an important life skill. How it works is that you deflect the parental unit's attention from you to something, or someone, else.

"Yeah, I'll never do that again," I said hurriedly. I really meant that. Having your head in a toilet bowl all night is not my idea of fun.

"I'm glad you're here, Mom," I continued, "because there is something I want to talk to you about. I think Sophia is getting cold feet. I heard her say she didn't want to marry Anthony after all."

"What?" Dad roared.

See? That was an example of a good distraction, because Dad immediately forgot me and focused on all of that wedding money going down the drain.

He left my bedroom at a run. "Sophia," I heard him shout.

"She probably just needs to talk to you, Mom. Brides and their nerves," I said. Wedding jitters 101.

"Yes. I'm sure she does." Mom said that with a small smile. Do you think she was on to me? She leaned down and kissed my forehead. "You're very special. And devious."

As Mom went out of the room, I noticed how big her stomach was getting with Boo-Boo. How on earth does skin stretch that far without ripping? Elastowoman.

I pulled Barbie and Ken out from under the blankets. "Hey, I get to date," I told them. "Except it's with the wrong guy."

r is For ReLАtionships
(don't have them!)

Monday started out bad. Really bad.

I slammed my locker door, looked up, and found myself boxed in by the Glams. Ashleigh pushed her face right into mine.

"Okay, I got you Greg. You were supposed to get me Hugo."

"You wanted me to bring Hugo to the party and I did," I said.

"The point of bringing Hugo was so that he could meet me and ask me out." Ashleigh poked me in my sock chest. Hopefully she was so mad she didn't feel the softness!

The Glams crowded in even closer. Kara's *brains* pushed up against my arm. (Seriously, they really are that big.) I shrank back, feeling the cold metal of my locker through my shirt.

"I can't make him like you," I said.

A collective gasp from the Glams.

"Excuse me? I never have to make anyone like me. They just do," Ashleigh said. She punctuated every word with a poke to my stomach this time.

"Well, maybe there was no chemistry," I said. "That's beyond my control."

Ashleigh's face clouded over. Obviously chemistry was something else Ashleigh naturally had.

"Or maybe he's gay," I added hastily. "His hockey equipment all matches."

"It's a team uniform! It's supposed to match," Melanie said.

I glared at her. Wasn't she supposed to be the dumb one?

"Hey, babe, did you miss me?"

Greg was grinning over Kara's shoulder. I looked around to see who he was talking to, then realized it was me. I was "babe." And right now, he was my knight in shining armor saving me from the evil witch. I wriggled out between Ashleigh and Kara. Greg put an arm around me. It really was beginning to look more and more like he might be my boyfriend.

"*Bonjoor*," he said.

"Hi." Some people shouldn't try to be what they aren't. Greg was definitely not multilingual.

Ashleigh flipped on her *a boy is near* switch, tossed her hair and smiled widely. "Did you get in trouble for having the party?" she asked.

"My parents were pretty pissed at me," Greg said. "And babe, that wine you drank? Cost my dad a hundred dollars for a bottle." He bent over double, laughing.

Wonder what his dad would have thought about the hundred-dollar wine being flushed down the toilet.

The bell rang. "Gotta run. See you at lunch, babe." Greg leaned down and planted a peck on my lips.

Boyfriends do that, right? Not just good friends, but *boy*friends. I think it's official. I have a boyfriend.

I tried to make my own getaway right behind him, but Ashleigh grabbed my arm. "You better arrange another meeting between Hugo and me. Or else."

You know, if she was going to keep threatening people, she was really going to get into some serious trouble with the law. But I didn't tell her that.

I got through the morning intact. At lunch, Greg led me through the cafeteria line to the prime AN tables. Despite Ashleigh glaring at me the entire time, it felt pretty great. I was part of the in-crowd, or in this case, the AN crowd. Well, it was great until Greg knocked Phillip's tray off the table as we passed. And when he walked by Talia, he snorted like a pig.

I tried to make myself small, so no one would see me. It almost felt like *I* had done those mean things—but I hadn't. Still, I could have *said* something. Damn my conscience.

Am I a bad person for wanting to be with the ANs? I mean, I'm not responsible for Greg's behavior, am I?

Elizabeth would probably say I was selling myself out to be popular. But wouldn't she and Phillip and Talia do the same thing in my position? Don't throw any stones at the glass house until you've walked a mile in my shoes.

I came out of my musings to hear Greg say, "You coming to my hockey game after school, babe? All the other girlfriends will be there."

Okay, understand that I hate hockey. Except the Zamboni thing that cleans the ice. It's kind of cool.

Why I Hate Hockey:
1. It's played in a COLD arena.
2. I hate arenas.
3. I hate arena odor. Sweaty hockey equipment, the sour smell of butter-saturated popcorn and fatty sausages. It makes me queasy.
4. I hate freezing to death. I hate my feet going numb from cold, losing feeling in my fingertips, and my nose turning red and dripping.

But as it seems as I am now a girlfriend, I guess I have to like hockey. They say life can change in the blink of an eye and I, for one, believe it. One moment I was hate-hockey-sports T and now I'm girlfriend-to-jock-love-hockey babe.

"Sure," I said.

A jab in my ribs. Ashleigh. Of course. Hugo would be playing too. "Can Ashleigh come?"

I was going to have to keep Greg for a boyfriend after all. He was the only thing standing between me and annihilation.

• • • • •

In History class, Elizabeth sat in front of me but she never turned around once. That was a good thing because if she had turned around, I would have given her a piece of my mind. I couldn't believe I used to think she was a friend. I ignored her right back, which isn't hard to do when you're being ignored. In fact, I'm not sure who was ignoring who first.

I told Mr. Timber that Grandma T and Nannu had agreed to speak. He went on again about "living history" and the "emotional impact of war," then added that I still had to hand in a written report. That was a bit of a downer. Still, I was feeling pretty happy with myself. Until the bell rang to end class and I stood up and gathered my books, and found myself face-to-face with Elizabeth.

"So you're one of them now?" she said.

"They're very nice people once you get to know them," I replied. "Better than some people who pretend to be friends, then show their true colors."

"What are you talking about?"

"You know what I'm talking about. Adam! You wanted him for yourself, so you sabotaged me."

"What?"

I have to admit, she gave a pretty good impression of surprise, but I was on to her.

"You think I'm like that? You think I'm that sort of person?" she said flatly. "I guess we're finished then."

She pushed past me. *Well, two can play at that game,* I thought. I started to push past her, but it's actually impossible to push past someone who has already pushed past you and is heading out the door. I was left staring at the back of her head.

All that staring and fuming made me late for gym. Inside the locker room, Talia was pulling a T-shirt over her head. It suddenly struck me that I'd never seen her change into her gym clothes before. She must wait until the room is nearly empty.

"Hi, Talia," I said glumly. I flopped onto the wooden bench and pulled my gym shoes out of my bag. I was so busy wallowing in misery that I didn't even realize I'd said hello to an SN.

But someone noticed.

"You and BB friends now?"

I hadn't even seen Melanie. She must have come out of one of the bathroom stalls.

I stood up, stuck my chin out, and said, "Yeah. What's it to you? I'll say hello to anyone I like."

Okay, that was the fantasy.

What I really said was, "Uh, no, I was saying hi to everyone. You know, like, "Hi, everybody in the room."

Except there were only the three of us.

I heard a snort of disgust from behind me. You know you have reached a real low when even the SNs look down on you.

"Yeah, right," Melanie said. She pulled open the gym door and left.

A minute later Talia went, too, but not before she threw me a scornful glance.

I changed into my gym shorts and discovered I had my period. Bloody (England-English) hell! Gym is horrible when you feel fine, but it's a nightmare when you have your period.

Multiple *thuds* of basketballs hitting the floor reached my ears when I opened the gymnasium door. Another dumb game. Throw the ball through a hoop suspended from the ceiling and everyone cheers. A rocket scientist must have thought of that one.

I stood at the side of the gymnasium, hoping Miss Cook wouldn't notice me. Suddenly, a basketball caught me full in the face. I fell flat on my back.

"Watch those balls, girls," Miss Cook shouted.

I lay for a moment on the hardwood floor, winded, feeling my tender nose.

"On your feet, Tolliver!" Miss Cook yelled. "Shake it off."

I slowly got up.

Merde! (French). Miss Cook was a *hamar* (Maltese).

Kara ran past. "Ashleigh says she's sorry. The ball got away from her."

I struggled through gym class, and then remembered that I, my period, my broken nose, and Ashleigh had to go to a freezing arena and watch a hockey game.

Okay, HP! I get the message! I've been bad!

After supper I gave Barbie and Ken a rundown of my dreadful day (Barbie suggested I put ice on my nose to stop the swelling) and how Ashleigh cheered loudly at the hockey game any time Hugo got the puck—so embarrassing. And also about how she promised she would pulverize me if Hugo didn't go out with her. I did leave out the part about my confronting Elizabeth with taking my almost-boyfriend.

First Truth I Did Not Want to Admit: I wanted to pretend that that part had never happened, because I felt a bit ashamed of myself. I had sort of jumped to conclusions about Adam and Elizabeth, and it was Adam who liked Elizabeth, according to Greg. And Elizabeth had never betrayed me our entire best-friendship. She'd been, well, Biff. It wasn't one of my better moments, and I saw no need to open myself to criticism from Barbie and Ken.
Second Truth I Did Not Want to Admit: I missed Eliza...Biff, a lot. A ton of lot.

But one problem at a time, and I needed to focus on the most important one. How to keep me alive and in one piece? I was tired of worrying. I needed a distraction.

"You know," I said to Barbie and Ken, "you two are

together all the time. You should get married before something happens."

This would take my mind off my problems. A wedding.

I rummaged through my old toy box and found Barbie's princess outfit—it could do double duty as a wedding dress. The only thing I could find for Ken was a pair of swimming trunks. So it would be a beach wedding. But first, Barbie got to stomp around.

Barbie: I want white flowers. No, red flowers. No, white flowers. I need to find the pukiest-green dress ever for my maid of honor. No one is allowed to look better than me. Because it's all about Me! Me! Me!

Then the solution to my problem hit me.

Fact: While you are not actively thinking about a problem, the brain continues to work, mulling it over and then, when you least expect it, a light bulb moment occurs. Seriously, try it.

I was making the problem way more complicated than it needed to be. It was simple. Just ask Hugo to ask Ashleigh out, subtly.

Hugo was on the computer in the living room.

I sauntered over. "So, Ashleigh enjoyed your hockey game," I said.

Note: See how I was subtle?

Hugo grunted. I took that as a sign of interest.

"She's pretty, don't you think?" I asked.

Note: Continuing with the subtle plan. Seems to be working.

"She's an airhead," Hugo said.

"Really?" I expressed my disbelief and crossed my fingers behind my back. "I've found that she's quite intelligent once you get to know her."

"Well, yeah, compared to you she's a genius," Hugo said.

The things I have to put up with.

"Why are you hanging around with her, anyway? Where's Biff?"

"Elizabeth is busy," I said shortly. "Besides, Ashleigh's lots of fun. She thinks you're really nice. You should ask her out," I said.

"Nope." Hugo packed up his books and stood up.

I spun his chair around, grabbed the front of his shirt and shook him, hard.

Note: Forget subtle if it appears not to be working.

"You have to go out with her. Just one date. Be yourself. Your usual, disgusting self. She'll never want to go out with you again. But you have to go out with her or I'm not getting any older."

"Are you pimping for her?" Hugo uncurled my fingers from his shirt.

"One date," I pleaded. "I'll do your chores for a month." Oh, oh, that was too hasty. "I mean, a week. Hugo, I'm desperate here. She's going to kill me if you don't go out with her."

"That's your problem." He left the room.

There was only one person to blame for the mess I was in—HP. If I'd been born popular, none of this would be happening.

19

s is For SeSS (Maltese)
Sex (English)
ShAgging (England-English)

Remember when I said the brain keeps working even when you aren't consciously thinking of something? Well, sometimes that's a pain in the *hamar*. Like at around midnight.

I tossed and turned while my brain kept me awake. Here are some of the random thoughts it insisted on having.

2:00 a.m.: I can never have sex! I'm allergic to condoms. So what is morally right? Tell a boy immediately that I'm allergic to latex so he knows up front he won't be getting any from me? Or wait until he knows my mind and my personality and loves me for myself and not for sex?

3:00 a.m.: From now on I'll wear shapeless beige sweaters and baggy camouflage pants so I won't give off sex vibes. It wouldn't be fair, and I'd be known as a tease.

4:00 a.m.: Nightmare. In the throes of passion with a faceless boy, I surface from a deep, lingering lip-lock. He whips out a *condiment.* "Sorry," I say. "No can do. Allergic, you know."

5:00 a.m.: I will never "know" a man, in the biblical sense. Well, I could, but then I would get PREGNANT.

6:00 a.m.: Sex is too much of a hassle. I'm joining a convent.

Why can't my brain have these enlightening discussions between, say, noon and four o'clock?

At breakfast I said, "Mom, Dad, just thought you should know. I'm becoming a nun."

"That will save us some money," Dad said. "One less wedding to bankrupt me."

"Nanna will be pleased. She's always wanted a nun in the family," Mom said dreamily.

I stared at Mom. Wasn't she supposed to ask me if I wanted to talk to *someone?* She just sat there looking all spaced out. Boo-Boo had hijacked all Mom's nurturing for herself. I decided to bring Mom's attention back to her previous children.

"I don't feel too good," I said.

I waited for Mom's hand on my forehead.

"You're going to be late for school," she said.

It was official. She no longer cared about me.

Sophia came storming into the kitchen and pointed a finger at me. "You've been in my room again, you freak!"

"No, I haven't," I protested. And this time I was telling the truth.

"Oh, that was me," Mom said. "I was measuring it up so I can decide where to put the crib."

"I haven't even left yet," Sophia shouted. "If I'd known you wanted me out of here, I would have moved out ages ago."

"Whatever you think best, dear," Mom said.

Obviously she didn't care about Sophia either. This was a dreadful turn of events. Unconcerned, Hugo kept shoveling in cereal. Food was all the attention he needed.

"She's nesting," Dad said.

All three of us kids stared in shock at Mom. I pictured her with little bits of feathers and straw, building a nest for Boo-Boo.

"All women go through it during the last few months of their pregnancy," Dad continued. "They prepare for their baby."

We transferred our shocked stares to Dad. How did he know about stuff like nesting?

"We've had three babies already," Dad said, by way of explanation.

Too bad I wasn't talking to Biff—wait, I mean Elizabeth. She'd love the entire nesting thing.

There really wasn't much to say after that nesting insight, so we all went our various ways. I left for school, tripped over D and D's hockey sticks on our front porch, plunged into a snowdrift, and hauled myself out. Just another morning in my sad, sad world.

I was so glad it was Friday. Being an AN's girlfriend was exhausting work. Always having to look good, smiling until your cheeks ached, tossing your hair, being perky. It was also expensive. New clothes, mascara, all these luxury items. I was babysitting so much these days that D and D thought I was their sister. Believe me, being in the popular group is not all it's cut out to be.

Today was a repeat of every day of the past two weeks: avoiding Ashleigh—which was hard to do now that I was at the AN cafeteria table—and when I couldn't avoid her, assuring her that Hugo was going to call her but he was busy with studying, hockey, household chores (take your pick, as I kept recycling the excuses).

At the same time I avoided Elizabeth (she made me feel uncomfortable) and ignored Phillip's moony eyes. And on top of that, I also had to do everything girls, well, *do* for their boyfriends. (Not that! Get your mind out of the gutter. Latex allergy, remember?) I mean, being supportive, laughing at his *stupidu* jokes, the hockey thing, waiting for him in the hall so we could walk together. If I had known how much work was involved, would I still have wanted a boyfriend so badly? I would have to search my soul for an answer to that.

Soul-Searching Elapsed Time: Ten seconds. Answer: Yes.

And all the time I was with Greg, I kept wishing it was AAA's arm around my shoulder. Every time I saw AAA, a pang shot through my heart. Was I an evil person for keeping a boyfriend I didn't really want just for the sake of having a boyfriend? I'd also have to search my soul for an answer to that.

Second Soul-Searching Elapsed Time: One entire minute. I really did mull over this one. Answer. Any girl would do the same thing in my situation. The truth is that having a boyfriend increases your popularity rating immeasurably.

This was real social work, much more difficult than the social work that helps the needy. Most evenings at home were spent talking to Greg on the phone (or on MSN when Mom told me to get off the phone), trying to wear Hugo down so he'd ask Ashleigh out, and babysitting for the cash needed to maintain my new status, while somehow I still had to do school work like my History paper. Exhausting.

But it was finally Saturday, and tonight Greg and I were going on our first official date—to the movies. I skipped supper, as I needed all the time available to get ready, and took over the bathroom for a couple of hours. The only problem was my stupid bra. But I didn't have time or money to replace it. Why? See below.

Cause and Effect: Another scientific theory I can apply to my situation.

Cause: As the girlfriend of a male AN, I have to have new clothes all the time.

Effect: I'm broke. As no one can see my inner clothes, I spend all my money on outer clothes rather than a new bra. Thus, I am still stuffing a sock into my bra.

I poked and prodded the sock into shape to look like a breast. (Yeah, I know that sounds weird.) I put on some lip gloss as the doorbell rang, ran into Mom's room and did a quick check of the entire ME in her full-length mirror (I looked hot), and took the steps downstairs two at a time so I could get to the door before anyone else.

Unfortunately, Hugo beat me to it, and his big body filled the front hall. "Hey, man," he said to Greg. Then he stood back and smirked.

I smacked his arm as I led Greg into the living room. This was the first time Mom and Dad were to meet "my young man." Except it wasn't just Mom and Dad who were there to meet him. I stopped in the doorway and my mouth fell open. While I was upstairs getting ready, the entire family had arrived to check out my boyfriend. Sophia and Anthony, Hugo, Nanna and Nannu, Aunt Grace and Aunt Connie, cousins—I couldn't even register all the other people in the room. I swear Mom and Dad had pulled strangers off the street to meet my boyfriend. Greg looked a little dazed to see all these people staring at him.

I took a deep breath. *"Maman, Papa, je m'appelle Greg,"* I said.

Honestly, I never know what is going to come out of my mouth.

"Greg, may I present my mother and father, my Nanna and Nannu, my sister Sophia and her fiancé, Anthony, if he doesn't get cold feet and leave her at the altar."

Anthony laughed, but quickly sobered up when Sophia glared at him.

"And of course, your mate, Hugo the *hamar*."

Nannu snickered, and Mom sent me a warning glance.

"Along with other assorted relatives too numerous to name," I finished.

I did a pretty good job considering the circumstances, didn't I?

Mom struggled to get up from her chair, but soon gave up and stayed put. Dad did get to his feet (his paunch is slightly smaller than Mom's), pumped Greg's hand, and kept pumping while his mind searched for something to say. We waited awhile but nothing came to him, and he finally dropped Greg's hand and sank back into the sofa, speechless.

"So, you take out my *namata*," Nannu said.

Greg looked puzzled.

"He's talking about me," I whispered to Greg. "That's Maltese for 'sweetheart.'"

"You better treat her right," Nannu went on. "I know all about pigs."

Pigs? Had Nannu just called Greg a pig?

"You can cut the tail off a pig, but it is still a pig,"

Nannu said. "I know about boys like you. I have five daughters. Five."

"Pa!" Mom and Nanna said in unison.

"So, where are you two kids going this evening?" Mom asked, trying to distract us from Nannu.

"We are going to the movies," I said.

"Did you use the medication for your rash, Teresa dear?" Sophia said. "We don't want it getting worse, now, do we?"

Getting back at me for the "left at the altar" comment, no doubt.

"She's just kidding," I hastily assured Greg. "It was just a little rash."

Greg looked stunned, and I suddenly saw my family through his eyes. My dad, a mute; Mom, pregnant in her forties; the two garden gnomes perched on the couch, one glaring and calling him a pig; Sophia frowning; Anthony panicked and desperately wondering if he could get out of the marriage; Hugo smirking in the background; and everyone else smiling and staring at us. My family was a freak show.

Omigawd! What if Greg tells AAA about my family?

"Goodness, look at the time!" I glanced down at my watchless wrist and gave Greg a shove toward the door. "We'd better get going if we don't want to miss the beginning of the movie," I said.

Greg's feet were rooted to the carpet. I pushed him harder and he staggered toward the door. I grabbed my coat.

"Remember your curfew," Mom called. Oh yeah, now she gets the caring gene back. Just in time to embarrass me!

"A pig!" Nannu shouted after us.

"I'm adopted," I told Greg as we went down the steps.

Greg had his dad's car, very nice and shiny, and he even held the door open for me. I slid in gracefully, feeling like a lady, and he closed the door on my skirt. It only got a bit of grease on it. We headed for Cinema House.

We didn't say a word all the way to the theatre. I mean, what was there to say after that sideshow?

We stood in the ticket line and it felt pretty great to be in line with a GUY, especially when there were all these DATE-LESS girls standing around. I know Greg is a moron and a bully, but hey, it was Friday night and I was out on a date. Perhaps I could work on his behavior. He'd learn, from my example, how to be tolerant of people, and he and I would break down the class structure at school together. We might even be Queen and King at the prom our senior year.

The lights went out as the previews lit up the screen, and that's when Greg's lips became glued to mine, and stayed that way for two hours until the movie ended and the lights came back on.

"Did you enjoy the movie?" he asked on the way out.

"*Wah, dono, no chans see.*" I'd just experienced my first serious make-out session and had the swollen lips to prove it.

"That was a great car chase at the end there," Greg said.

How on earth did he see that? Was he kissing with his eyes open? Omigawd! Do I look weird when I kiss?

I sank back into the leather seat of the car, puzzled. Something was missing. We'd kissed through the entire movie. Shouldn't I be feeling something?

What Movies Say about Kissing: Fireworks, earth moving, rising music.

What I Say about Kissing: Swollen lips, popcorn bits between teeth (I hope they're mine), but no fireworks. Not even a fizzle. Nada. (Spanish) Omigawd, I was a lesbian or frigid. So that's how the HP was going to handle my latex allergy.

We had only driven a short distance when Greg pulled off at a gravel pit and parked. Every stalker, axe/chainsaw-murderer urban myth came out of the dark to haunt me. I didn't really like this place. Before I could say anything, though, he climbed into the back seat, pulling me over with him (that was not easy) and reattaching his lips to mine.

What Movies Say about Kissing, Part II: Soulful looks. In movies, the girl and boy look deeply into each other's eyes; he tenderly strokes her cheek, tells her she's beautiful, THEN the lip-lock.

Us: Wrestling around in the back seat, going from zero to a thousand: bypassing lingering looks, tender cheek stroking, or whispered compliments. It was like being attached to a vacuum cleaner. Serious suction.

I had a moment of panic when I couldn't breathe, but in time remembered I had a nose. So, I decided, if I had to be in a lip-lock, I'd take advantage of the moment to try really hard to feel something…anything.

Greg didn't seem to be having any trouble. He moaned and called me babe, and slurped all over my face, and generally seemed to be enjoying himself at a one-man party. Surely there was a little spark somewhere in all that for me? And should my brain be thinking about all this stuff during a make-out session? Concentration. That's what was needed here.

I set my mind to concentrating, and perhaps if I hadn't concentrated so hard, what happened next wouldn't have happened, and the whole rest of my life wouldn't have been totally destroyed!

It took me a moment to become aware that Greg's hand was fumbling underneath my sweater at the back. A *sproing*, and my bra came loose. I felt his hand come around my side, zeroing in on, yes, he was heading for the boobs! I yelped and pushed him away, and we separated with a loud sucking noise.

Greg pulled his hand from under my sweater and stared at it. "What the hell is this?"

He held up a sock. My sock!

"Omigawd! Give me that!" I grabbed it out of his hand.

Things I Thought of After
1. I should have denied any knowledge of the sock.
2. I should have asked him why he was taking off his socks in the car.
3. Static cling. Must have been stuck in my top. I'm always telling my mom to use fabric softener.
4. Sock? What sock?

What I Did: I threw the sock in my purse and quickly did up my bra.

"Did you have that stuffed in your bra?" he asked.

"Of course not." I snorted with disgust.

"Yes, you did." He started to laugh. No, not just laugh, but roll all over the car seat holding his sides.

"I'd like to go home now," I said, mustering up as much dignity as possible. I crawled back into the front seat and crossed my arms over my chest to hide the lop-sidedness.

Greg laughed all the way to my house. I got out with a frosty, "Good night." It sounded like, "goognigh." (Swollen lips, remember?) I didn't make it to the door, though, before I started to cry.

Mom was already in bed, and Dad, who had waited up for me, snored in the armchair. I stifled my sobs and tiptoed past him up the stairs to my room. I didn't want to tell anyone of my date disaster. I grabbed Ken off my dresser and pitched him into the closet and kicked a pile of dirty clothes over him. I was finished with men. Real or plastic.

Barbie and I crawled into bed and pulled the covers over our heads. She listened quite sympathetically while I cried and told her what happened, but I knew she didn't really understand. How could she, when she has a perfect life with her perfect convertible and perfect Dream House and perfect plastic boobs?

t is For tRouBLe

Sunday morning, after my disastrous date, I wandered into the bathroom, glanced in the mirror, and did a double-take! Omigawd! On my neck! A HUGE PURPLE HICKEY! I didn't even remember getting it! I clapped a hand over it and ran from the bathroom to my bedroom, where I quickly pulled on a turtleneck sweater.

I told Mom I wasn't feeling too good, which with my swollen lips (kissing), swollen eyes (crying), and huge hickey was the truth. I must have looked pretty bad, because she didn't even insist I go to church and to Aunt Grace's for the afternoon. She did ask me if there was anything I wanted to talk about with her or *someone.* Nope!

Sophia popped in and pulled the neck of my sweater down before I could stop her. "Hmmm. Try lemon juice."

"You mean, like, drink lemonade?" I said.

She rolled her eyes. "No *stupidu*. Dab that … that *thing* on your neck with lemon juice. Supposedly it helps leech out the redness."

Internet Research: Hickeys are caused by suction on the neck that breaks blood vessels beneath the skin, leaving a red welt. Hickeys are marks of possession. Some girls display them proudly as a way of saying, "I am his."

Well, according to the Internet, it seems that hickeys are sort of like a boy branding you as his. It's like marking cows so you know which ranch they belong to. Actually, I don't think I like that whole cow comparison thing. I'm not sure about belonging to a boy. I mean, I want a boyfriend, but *belonging to him?* Like a shirt, or CD or some other possession?

I slept a lot. Which I liked, because being unconscious meant not remembering. But in my waking moments I had time to think about socks, Monday, boys, socks, school, bras, and socks, and that was when I decided I wasn't ever going back to that dumb school.

About mid-afternoon I raided Mom's stash of peanut butter cups—her latest craving—and chewed while rubbing half a lemon on my neck. It didn't seem to make a difference to the welt, though I smelled quite nice in a citrusy sort of way. And so the day passed.

• • • • •

"Mom," I said at breakfast on Monday morning. I took a gulp of orange juice for courage and fingered my neck to make sure it was covered by my sweater. "I have decided that the traditional school setting is not doing a very good job of educating me. I could do better by taking online courses. And you'll be home soon with Boo-Boo, and you could home-school me."

Mom's eyebrows flew up at that.

"I could probably get my diploma even sooner without all the distractions of the modern-day high school, like drugs in the halls. It's a dangerous environment for a sensitive teen, and if you only knew how little time was actually spent on school work … well, it's very little." I let her digest that fact for a moment.

I pointed to a pile of books I'd brought down. "I'm quite disciplined, so I'll have no difficulty working on my own. In fact, I'll get started right now, which means I'm actually studying before real school even begins." See? Fine example of self-discipline.

"Aren't Grandma and Nannu coming to your History class today?" Mom asked

Oh crap! My History project. I'd completely forgotten that was today. Perhaps I could phone them and head them off…

"Teresa, go to school," Mom said gently. "Whatever it is that's bothering you, it won't be as bad as you think."

Note to the Uninformed: If anyone ever tells you it won't be as bad as you think, don't believe them. It's always worse.

I walked to school by myself, flat as a pancake, in spirit and also physically. Greg had broken the snap of my air-bra, so I was forced to wear my old one—underneath three sweaters, hoping the bulk would disguise my shortcomings. Thank goodness it was snowing because I could also wear my parka. This was the last week of classes before Christmas break.

Besides, I told myself as I trudged through mud-colored slush, no one was going to know about the sock-in-the-bra thing. Surely Greg was enough of a gentleman not to tell his friends. Right? I almost had myself convinced by the time I hit the school doors.

The bell rang as I ran down the hallway to my locker. Why were there so many people still in the hall? I pushed my way forward and had my answer soon enough.

They were there to see MY LOCKER! Someone had decorated it—WITH SOCKS! I could only stare. It was like a garish nightmare: hoots and hollers, Ashleigh grinning broadly, the Glams giggling, Greg, yes Greg, doubled-over laughing. I couldn't breathe. I was going to pass out.

"To your classes! *Maintenant!*" M. Papineau came out of the classroom and clapped his hands twice.

An arm reached past me and grabbed a sock from my locker. "Idiots." It was Talia.

A second hand grabbed another sock. Elizabeth. She and Talia stripped the socks from the locker. Elizabeth dumped them into my arms without a word and went into class before I could even thank her.

I shoved the socks in my locker, grabbed my books, gritted my teeth, and went into homeroom. No way was I letting Ashleigh and the Glams get to me. And Greg? I was dumping him.

Note to the Uninformed: It is always better to be the dumper than the dumpee. Always try to dump before you get dumped, even it if means dumping before you even feel you're at that point. Because believe me, there is always that point, and you may as well make the first move.

Greg could go suck on some other girl's neck.

I got through the morning announcements and headed to our first class, History. We sat in silence for eight minutes. I was wringing my hands by now. Where were Grandma T and Nannu?

Finally Mr. Timber said, "Until Teresa's grandparents arrive, we'll do a pop quiz."

Everyone groaned and glared at me. This day was just getting better. I couldn't figure out why they were late. I'd given Nannu detailed instructions on how to get to the school. He was to pick up Grandma T on the way, so I had given her directions also as a backup. Had they both forgotten?

As we pulled out our notebooks, the office buzzed: *"Could Teresa Tolliver come down. Her guests are here."*

Saved by the … um … buzzer.

I hurried them down the hall to History class. Grandma T muttered under her breath the entire time: " … one way streets ... stop signs are there for a reason ... nearly got us killed ... "

Nannu walked into the classroom, beamed at everybody, and noisily sorted his slides into the projector carousel.

Grandma T began with a prim "Good morning, girls and boys."

Snickers greeted that. I squirmed in my seat. My History grade was doomed. My life was doomed. Mom had to home-school me.

Then ...

"Imagine a dark night. There are no lights allowed because of the blackout. Suddenly, the drone of an engine, a plane, then more and more until the sky is full, except you can't see them, because it is so black."

The room was completely quiet.

"You run down the stairs of your house and into the garden, but before you can make it to the bomb shelter ... "

Hey, she was good. Really good.

" ... the sky lights up, there is a terrible *whoosh* of wind and heat and light, and the windows of the house behind you explode, scattering glass shards everywhere."

I heard an intake of breath. Grandma T had them in the palm of her hand.

"That is what we in England endured night after night throughout the war."

WOW! I was going to get a fabulous mark in History this term.

Grandma T went on to tell them how it felt to be evacuated from her home and have to live with strangers.

Then it was Nannu's turn. I relaxed. No worries here. Everyone would love Nannu.

He asked that someone "close the lights, please."

The first slide showed an overview of Malta, and Nannu explained how tiny an island Malta is but how important a role it played in the war as a safe haven in the Mediterranean for the Allies until the Germans came and bombed it and blockaded their supplies to starve them. He showed the limestone caves where he and his family stayed during the bombing. Another slide came up. "This … this … " Silence.

After a few minutes, Mr. Timber turned on the lights. "Is there a problem?" he asked.

Nannu stood blinking, taking in the class in front of him. He looked … lost. He fired off a long string of Maltese.

I went to him and shook his arm. "Nannu?"

"Fiona." And he spoke rapidly in Maltese again. I couldn't tell exactly what he was saying, but I think he thought I was Mom, and he was asking where Nanna was.

"Nannu. It's me, Teresa."

He looked right at me, and my heart stopped. There was no recognition in his eyes.

Grandma T gently pulled me back.

"Mr. Psaila isn't feeling too well, girls and boys. I do hope you enjoyed our talk." She took Nannu's arm and led him to the hall.

"Teresa, dear, please call your mother. Tell her your grandfather isn't feeling too well and we need a lift home," Grandma ordered calmly.

I ran to the office and used the phone. I tried to be like Grandma, calm, when I spoke to Mom, but halfway through I lost it and began to cry. Then I asked the secretary to find Hugo for me. Tears washed down my face.

Grandma T came in with Nannu.

"Teresa, why you crying?" Nannu asked.

He knew me. What on earth was going on?

He looked around the office, then focused on the secretary. "You make her cry?" he demanded.

"I think the stories of the war upset her," Grandma T said. "She's at a very sensitive age."

Hugo came charging in. "What's going on?"

Nannu said, "Who this boy? He make you cry?"

Hugo stared at Nannu.

Grandma T patted his arm. "Your grandfather isn't feeling well. Your mother's on her way. Perhaps a cup of tea?" Grandma T said to the secretary.

The secretary started, then scurried off to do Grandma's bidding. She returned a few minutes later with a tray loaded with cups and saucers and a teapot, and led us into the principal's office.

And that's how Mom and Dad found us. Having a Mad Hatter's tea party in the principal's office, with Grandma pouring.

u is For ugly

E-mail
Monday 8:30 p.m.
To: GLAMGRRL1
From: T
Subject: Date with Hugo

> Hugo says you are a complete airhead and he wouldn't go out with you if you were the last female on earth. Tossing your DYED hair around so much has given you brain damage, Ashleeeee.

OMIGAWD! I hit *send!* I meant to hit *delete!* Instead, I hit *send!* It was just a venting e-mail, not a real one! Now I'd really done it. Not only was my life in the toilet—but I'd just flushed it!

Tuesday: "WHORE" was painted right across my locker. M. Papineau and the vice-principal wanted to know if I knew who had done it. I widened my eyes, and told them that someone must have got my locker by mistake and it was really meant for someone else. Though who, I added hastily, I had no idea.

Wednesday: E-mails started to come. From people I didn't even know! They called me a skank, slut, bitch, and whore. Every time I read one of THOSE WORDS, it felt like I'd been slapped in the face.

Thursday: A rumor went around school that I'd gone ALL THE WAY with Greg. Which I HADN'T. I mean, things pretty much fell apart after that sock incident. Didn't people realize what a damper that is on passion? The rumors even penetrated Hugo's dim brain and he wanted to know what was going on. I told him that what was going on was that he'd ruined my entire life by not asking Ashleigh out on one measly date.

Friday: At school today, Talia came up to my locker and said not to worry, that no one believed the rumors anyway. I couldn't believe I was being comforted by a SN! Who obviously thought I was also a SN! When I'm so obviously NOT! I might not be an AN anymore, but I had not sunk so far as SN. So, instead of being nice and thanking her, I snarled at her to get lost. Unfortunately, I didn't realize that Elizabeth and AAA were standing behind my locker door at the time. I slammed my door shut and there they were. They looked at me and left without saying a word. That did it. AAA had seen me at my worst. And he was with Elizabeth. He was lost to me forever. I have had a fall from grace of Biblical Proportions and there's only one person to blame—Hugo!

To Sum Up: Worst week of my life!

On top of it all, I was scared that Nannu was sick, really sick. He was in the hospital having tests. The doctors thought he might have had a stroke. Nanna was a mess. The aunts were a mess. And Mom was the biggest mess. She was worried sick about Nannu. And I do mean literally sick. Her blood pressure went sky-high and she was ordered to bed for the next week.

And worry over her turned Dad into a total mute. His power of speech was almost entirely gone now, even around us. Do you see how our lives impact on each other? Like a stone thrown in a pond, the ripples reach out farther and farther. (Just for the record, I didn't make that up. I read it somewhere in a self-help book. But it fits my life so well right now, I had to use it.)

Finally, it was Saturday morning and I didn't have to go to school for two whole weeks. Christmas break. Still, I was scared to open my e-mail. Or my front door. Or be near a window. I decided to spend the vacation in bed.

I grabbed a pen and paper and Barbie, and crawled under the covers. I'd write a list outlining my good and bad points and maybe studying it would help me make some sense out of my … well … senseless life.

What I Am—Bad Things
liar
sinner
ugly
unfriendly
snotty (like a snob, not a mucus thing)
whore (I had let Greg unfasten my bra, after all)
judgmental (the whole AN, N, SN thing)
ugly (yeah, I know it's there already, but I'm ugly
        inside AND out, so it needs to be there twice)
shallow
weak

Good Things
listmaker

I stared down at the list I had a made. A big fat tear smudged the ink. The only good thing about me was my listmaking ability.

I tossed Barbie across the room in a fit of anger. (Yes, you can add doll-killer to the bad list if you like.) The truth is that she was no comfort at all. She was hard, plastic, and perfect, and she just reminded me of how ugly I was in comparison.

"Teresa! Hugo!" Sophia called from downstairs.

Oh yeah, and then there was Sophia. We thought she

was bad in her Bride role? Well, she was even more psycho in her new role of Housekeeper. With Mom in bed, Sophia had appointed herself (no one would have voted her in, so she did it her way) Keeper of the House.

I dragged myself downstairs, reaching the kitchen at the same time as Hugo.

"What?" we both asked, suspiciously.

Sophia had been a pain in the *hamar* all week. She kept making lists (my specialty by the way, not hers!) of chores for me and Hugo to do. She proceeded to hand yet another list to Hugo and then one to me. I blinked. I *make* lists. I don't *receive* them!

"Now, these are the duties I have assigned to each of you for today so that Mom doesn't have to do anything."

Hugo and I stared at each other.

"I don't do laundry," Hugo said.

"Well, then you'll wear dirty clothes," Sophia told him.

Hugo shrugged. That didn't bother him.

I looked at my list.

"So I'm supposed to dust, vacuum, wash the kitchen floor..." And that was just the first three of about twenty "duties."

"So what exactly is left for you to do?" Hugo asked.

"I'm working the hardest," Sophia explained. "Those lists took a lot of organizational skills. Everyone knows a work team needs a supervisor to keep everything together."

I looked at my list again. "I want to be supervisor. I make great lists. I'll keep us organized."

"Well, you can't," Sophia said. "That position is already filled. You're in the labor position."

"But we didn't even get a choice," Hugo argued. "I want the supervisor position."

"As the oldest person here, the supervisor's position is mine," Sophia said.

"Well, speaking as the youngest person here, you can go—" I began.

"I'm the oldest person here. I'll take the supervisor position," a new voice said.

We all whipped around to see Grandma T in the doorway. Dad hovered behind her, carrying her suitcase.

"What was that you were going to say as youngest person, Teresa?" Grandma T asked.

You know, I swear I saw her lips briefly twitch with amusement.

"Nothing," I muttered.

Grandma T took the lists from us and scanned them, then sat at the table with a pen. "A cup of tea, please, Teresa dear, while I rewrite these lists. Everyone will have a *labor* position. Many hands make light work."

I never thought I'd look upon Grandma T as a savior, but she'd come to my rescue twice now. I filled up the tea kettle, sticking my tongue out at Sophia as I passed her on my way to get cups and saucers from the china cabinet. Grandma T would never drink from a mug.

Mom shuffled into the room in her slippers and housecoat. She gave Grandma T a peck on the cheek, then went to sit at the table. Hugo leaped forward to hold out a chair for her. Once Mom got over her shock at that gallant action, she said, "Grandma is going to stay with us over the Christmas holidays. You girls can double up in Sophia's room..."

Sophia's mouth gaped open.

"And Grandma will stay in yours, Teresa," Mom said. She took a deep breath. "I'm glad everyone is here because Dad and I want to talk to you."

Reminder: Remember how I said if Mom AND Dad talk to you, it's always bad.

I felt my stomach lurch.

"We've received the results of Nannu's tests. He has the early stages of Alzheimer's disease." Mom's voice wobbled.

"Nannu's going bonkers?" Hugo asked.

"No," Dad roared.

Mom took over. "Marshall, they don't have any information. Alzheimer's is a progressive disease that affects the brain, the memory, behavior, body functions." Mom swallowed back a sob and went on. "But recently there has been a lot of new research, and there are medications Nannu can take to slow the progress of the disease. And there are lots of ways that we can help him."

I didn't want to hear anymore. I got up and took the boiling kettle off the stove. I couldn't stand the thought of Nannu being sick. I rinsed out the pot with hot water (Grandma T nodded approvingly) and put in two teabags.

I knew about Alzheimer's from a movie I'd seen, about a writer who couldn't write anymore because her brain was so messed up, and writing was the only thing she loved to do. She got to the point where she didn't even recognize the people who were closest to her. Like Nannu hadn't recognized me in History class. I felt as if a black hole had opened up in front of me and I was falling in.

Mom was still explaining the changes we might see in Nannu, so I went through to the dining room and got our good sugar and creamer. If I didn't hear about it, maybe then Nannu's illness would just go away.

"So, we're all going to pitch in" (Grandma T was talking now), "so your Mom can get a good rest. Speaking of which, Fiona, you get into bed and Teresa will bring you some tea."

Mom meekly obeyed Grandma T. A few minutes later, I followed her upstairs with a cup of tea. I fluffed pillows and straightened sheets, hoping Mom would ask me if I needed *someone* to talk to. I did. But she stared out the window with her tea balanced on her bulging stomach, and I left.

I changed the sheets on my bed and grabbed my pajamas and slippers. Sophia was in her room when I went in, clearing out a drawer in her dresser.

"There," she said. "You can use that for your stuff. You have your own drawer, so you don't have to go into any of mine."

I wanted to make a joke about Anthony rifling through her drawers, but I felt too tired to even talk.

Sophia drew an imaginary line down the middle of the bed with one finger. "This side is mine and that..." she pointed to the side nearest the window. "is yours."

Seriously? How childish can a person be?

I sat on the edge of the bed—HER edge. "Oohhh look, I'm on YOUR side," I said.

She tackled me and pulled me off the bed to the floor. My slippers flew from my hand, hitting the wall with a *clunk*. Barbie fell out. Rats! I had hidden her in my one of the slippers.

"That doll is not sleeping in my bed," Sophia announced.

I grabbed Sophia's hair and yanked her to the floor with me.

"Be sure you draw a line so Anthony doesn't come over on your side," I said.

Sophia twisted my nose.

"OWWW! You broke my nose," I yelled. It was still sore from the basketball hit a few weeks ago.

"Sophia."

We both looked up to see Grandma T standing in the doorway.

"You have company."

Grandma T stepped aside and Anthony peered in.

"I believe that is your bride-to-be, on the floor wrestling with her sister," Grandma T said.

Anthony's mouth fell open.

I think I love Grandma T.

22

v is For Vengeance, Vendetta

(and no, not the obvious female anatomy thing. Grow up!)

Christmas Eve morning. We have a proper tree, properly lit and properly decorated. We have a proper wreath on our front door, and proper holiday cookies.

Proper Christmas Baking: shortbread, sugar cookies decorated with cherry centers, and mince-meat tarts. Nanna has other proper Maltese Christmas cookies.

While we did our proper Christmas baking, Grandma told us about Christmas in England during the war years, about sugar and butter rations, and how it felt to spend Christmas away from home with strangers. Oddly, I didn't mind that Grandma T insisted everything be done properly. It puts things in order, like my lists. I'll have to write a *Proper* list.

I'd stuck close to home the past week, except for the occasional foray next door to babysit D and D while their mother shopped for non-pointy, non-harmful toys for them for Christmas. I found myself pathetically grateful that D and D acted the same way toward me as they always did. I didn't even mind too much when they glued the back of my hair to the couch while I watched television. (I don't know who got the worst of that—me with glue in my hair, or the Middletons, who got my hair on their couch.) It felt normal.

It also didn't matter what I looked like these days, since I never left the house. I was back to wearing my old bra. Do you know how much time I wasted poking and prodding and worrying about that *&^%$ sock? A lot.

Not having a social life, I had a fair amount of money saved up for Christmas gifts. I couldn't think of a thing to get for Nannu, though I knew what I was getting Grandma T: a bone china cup and saucer. OMIGAWD! It just occurred to me that bone china might be made from, well, bone!

Internet Research: (Okay, this is gross. I am not making this up.) Bone china is made up of 25 percent china stone, 25 percent china clay, and 50 percent calcined cattle bones.

I think I'll get Grandma T a pottery mug. That's just made with dirt, not bones. And yes, I do appreciate the irony of the fact that I will eat cow, but won't eat *off* of cow. Maybe along with home-schooling, I'll become a vegetarian.

Grandma T was in the kitchen with Mom, who was now allowed up for a few hours each day and looking pretty much like her old self. I was sitting in my pajamas in front of the computer, terrified to turn it on yet wanting to look all the same. It was like driving past a car accident. You want to see the blood, but you don't want to see the blood. "A paradox in human nature, repulsed and yet fascinated at the same time," Biff would say. I felt my eyes tear up at the thought of Biff. I missed her so much. And she really was Biff, not Elizabeth like I had made her. But I'd deal with that guilt later. Time to download my very own car crash.

Steeling myself for the worst, I waited, but nothing happened. Only five e-mails in my box, four of which were junk and one from Talia.

E-mail
3:00 p.m.
To: T
From: BGGRL
Subject: Grandfather

> Hi Teresa,
> Just wanted to say that I hope ur grandfather is ok.
> Talia, proud to be a BGGRL

Where was all my hate mail? Was the get-Teresa vendetta over?

I don't know if it was relief or all the crap going on in my life at the moment, but reading Talia's e-mail sent tears streaming down my cheeks. She was the only person who wanted to know how Nannu was. I'd been wrong the whole time! She wasn't an SN. She was an AN. The whole system was upside down!

Hugo came up behind me. "I asked Ashleigh out so you wouldn't get any more e-mails."

"What?" I yelled. I wiped the tears from my face. "No way. You are not going out with that two-timing, back-stabbing..." I saw Grandma T in the kitchen and hastily swallowed the next word, substituting "witch."

Word I Meant to Say: Substitute "b" for "w." Okay, it's not nice, but it's what I wanted to say.

"You were the one telling me to ask her out," Hugo said. "She promised to stop the e-mails and the whole writing on your locker thing."

"No," I said. "You can't give in to her. That's a... it's a SIN."

"A sin?"

"Okay, not technically a sin, but you can't give way to someone who's bullying you. You don't like her. You shouldn't have to go out with her."

Hugo looked uncertain. "But it's my Christmas present to you," he said.

My heart melted for a moment, then rapidly solidified.

This was Hugo! "You don't have any money for Christmas gifts this year, right?"

Hugo looked as embarrassed as Hugo could possibly look.

"I thought of it as a gift from the heart." He clutched his chest.

"Oh puhleeze. You spent all your money on computer games or hockey stuff. Are you giving *heart gifts* to everyone? You're cheap. Well, I'm making you return my gift. I don't want it. Oops, no receipt. Whatever will you do?"

The doorbell rang.

"Ummm, that might be another gift for you," he said.

"What did you do?" I demanded.

Hugo went to the front door and yanked it open. Greg stepped in.

"Merry Christmas," Hugo said.

Omigawd! I was in my pajamas, my hair not combed, my face not washed—had I brushed my teeth? I ran a tongue over them—nope. Hugo was so dead.

"Hi babe," Greg said.

The nerve. "Don't you *babe* me, you jerk." I walked right up to Greg, despite my unbrushed teeth, and poked a finger in his chest. "You're a kiss-and-teller, except this time, it was a sock-finder-and-teller. I cannot believe you turning up here all nice and *hi babe*."

I saw Hugo inch his way toward the door. "Don't you go anywhere," I yelled.

"I just thought you'd want some privacy or something," Hugo muttered.

"Don't you want to see me open my gift?" I asked.

"I only told Ashleigh," Greg said.

"Ashleigh?" I swung back around. "You only told the biggest mouth in school?"

"She asked how the date went, and I thought it was funny so I told her. She said she wouldn't tell anyone."

Note to the Uninformed or Just Plain Dumb Like Greg: When someone pries a secret out of you by saying those infamous words, "I won't tell anyone," DO NOT BELIEVE THEM.

"It was cute. You're cute," Greg said.

True, I am, but that didn't matter. "And the socks all over the locker?"

"Her idea. I had no part in that."

"You laughed, Greg. It was embarrassing. Why didn't you stick up for me?"

"Yeah, I know. Adam and Hugo told me that. I'm sorry. It's just..." He leaned forward and whispered in my ear. "I'm not used to this boyfriend-girlfriend thing. I don't know what to do."

"Well, I'm not your girlfriend anymore, so problem solved," I said.

Greg looked utterly shocked. "Sure you are."

"No, I'm not." I pulled down my collar and pointed to my neck. "See? No brand."

"Brand?"

I turned on Hugo. "Why are you still here? Can't you see this is a private conversation?"

He ran for the kitchen door, where—guess what?—every member of my family except Grandma T was standing and listening.

"Grandma," I called.

She came down the stairs from the bedrooms and I gestured toward the doorway. She took in the situation immediately. "Righto dear," she said. "Everyone into the kitchen. It is not proper to listen in on a private conversation." She herded them before her and shut the door.

"Adam and Hugo told you it was wrong?" I asked.

"Yeah," Greg said earnestly. "I really am sorry, and I really like you and want you to be my girlfriend."

"I can't be the girlfriend of someone who is mean to other people and makes fun of them."

"Like Maggot?" Greg said.

"Yes, like Maggot." I shook my head. "No, Phillip. That's his name. Phillip."

You know, Greg is kind of hot. Especially standing there in my doorway, all humble and embarrassed. And a hedgehog in hand sure beats two hiding in the…ummm, cedar hedge or something like that (Nannu's saying). It's supposed to mean: go with what you have and stop wishing for something else.

But was that fair to Greg? Or to myself?

"I don't think I want to be anyone's girlfriend just

yet," I said slowly. It had to be slowly because I was thinking this all out in my own head as I spoke. If I'd only been pre-warned that Hugo was going to give me this *heart gift*, I would have had time to draw up a Pros and Cons Girlfriend List. Instead, I was just going to have to go with my gut instinct.

"I'd like to be friends, though," I said.

Can you believe this? What a whirlwind relationship. I was already at the breaking-up-but-we-can-be-friends stage.

"So you don't want to be *anyone's* girlfriend?" Greg asked.

"No. Not right now." And it was true. I didn't even want to be AAA's girlfriend. The truth is, I'd only admired him from afar. I hadn't even spoken to him. What I did want, though, was to be best friends with Biff again. If she would let me, that is. I wanted to wait a bit before I had a boyfriend. I was the youngest in my class, after all. I had time.

"Sure, we can be friends, then," Greg said.

"But I'm still being friends with Talia and Phillip," I said.

"Whatever. You got it, babe."

Yeah, we'd work on that babe thing later. I didn't want to overload Greg's brain too much.

"I got to go," Greg said. "We're heading out of town for Christmas. I'll call you when I get back, okay?"

"Yeah. I'd like that."

As he turned to leave, Nanna and Nannu pushed past him into the house, with Dad trailing behind.

"Is that the boy you like?" Nannu asked. "He likes you now?"

"I'm not having a boyfriend just yet, Nannu," I said.

I shoved Greg out the door before Nannu could call him a pig or Dad could ask him about snakes. As I shut the door behind him, I heard Greg trip over D and D's sled. I hoped he was okay, because I wasn't opening that door again. I'd had enough *gifts* for one day.

I ran upstairs to get dressed. I had lots to do, and it was pushing noon.

w is For Wimp, Wuss...
you get the idea

E-mail
12:50 p.m.
To: BGGRL
From: T
Subject: THX

Hi Talia,

Thx for asking about my Nannu (that's Maltese for Grandfather). He's doing better now, though he has Alzheimer's. But we're helping him out lots. I'm sorry I was so mean to you when you were being nice to me, and I promise I won't be anymore. And that's not just the Christmas spirit talking. I really mean it. Would you like to get together over the holidays and do something?
L8R T

Barbie and I had just made a list. It was time I walked the walk... or was that talked the walk? Walked the talk? Whatever. It was time.

List of Things to Do on Christmas Eve:
1. Apologize to Biff for being a jerk. I mean, ME being a jerk, not Biff. And ask her to be my friend again.
2. Thank and apologize to Talia, for reasons above.
3. Apologize to Phillip, same reason as above and above.
4. Get Christmas gifts for family and Biff, if she'll be my best friend again.

I logged out of my e-mail feeling very accomplished. Number 2 was crossed off my list.

Now for No. 1. Before I left, though, I headed to Mom's room. She was sitting up in bed, flipping through a magazine. The color was back in her face, the purple circles under her eyes gone.

"Mom," I said, "do *you* need *someone* to talk to? Because if you do, you can talk to me."

Tears shone in Mom's eyes. "Teresa, that is the nicest thing anyone has ever said to me. Come here, sweetie."

I cuddled up next to her on the bed, feeling like I was five years old. She put an arm around me.

"I'm sorry," she said.

"For what?" I asked.

"For not taking time to talk to you when I knew you

were going through some hard times. I just didn't have the energy, with Nannu sick and the baby and everything else going on. I let you down."

"No, you didn't," I assured her. "I am an adult now…" Well, not exactly *right* now, when I was lying all snuggled next to my mommy, but hey, I was trying. "And sometimes you have to deal with things yourself."

We lay quietly for a few minutes.

"Do you have a boyfriend still?" Mom asked.

"No. I thought I would just play the field. Date a whole bunch of different guys."

"There are lots of boys out there who'll want to date you."

Really? Well, where the heck were they? Certainly not lined up outside my door.

"I'm kidding, Mom. I don't want to date anyone right now. It's too exhausting and confusing."

"Well, when you're ready, be picky. Take only the best, like I did with your dad."

I snorted at that. Seriously? Dad was the best?

Mom poked me in the side. "Everyone has a few faults. Your father is very kind. You would be lucky to get someone like him."

We could hear Nanna and Grandma T talking downstairs. They were in the kitchen getting brunch ready for tomorrow morning. We would have Christmas dinner at Aunt Grace's. Grandma T was coming too, and afterwards she was going back to her own home. I'd miss her, but I was glad to be getting my bedroom back. Poor Anthony, having to share with Psycho Sophia. I felt a pang of pity for him, but only a little one. He had, after all, pushed food in my face when I was feeling under the weather—a.k.a. hungover.

But I didn't hear Nannu. Normally he would be the loudest in the house, teasing Nanna as she and Grandma T worked in the kitchen.

Mom must have been thinking the same thing. "Honey, you haven't talked much to Nannu since he came home from the hospital."

"I've been really busy with babysitting and Christmas shopping," I said.

"Too busy for Nannu? That doesn't sound like you."

I squirmed. "He needs rest and I didn't want to disturb him or make him tired or sick again," I added weakly.

How It Feels When I Think About Nannu: My chest gets tight, my eyes sting, my heart pounds and, for some reason, my lungs stop pumping so I have to gulp to get in air. Weird, huh?

I sat up. "I'm going over to Biff's."

Note: This is an avoidance tactic. Forget facing up to your problems. Cut and Run.

"It's about time you two made up," Mom said. "I wondered why she wasn't around much. You don't want to let a good friend go, Teresa. They're too few and far between. Hang on to your good friends as tight as possible."

"I will, Mom." I bent over and touched Mom's stomach. "Bye, Boo-Boo." And she kicked my hand. OMIGAWD! My sister knows me already and she's not even out here in the world yet. I'm going to be the best big sister ever.

As I grabbed my coat from the front hall closet, I turned and saw Nannu smiling at me. Expectantly. I think he wanted me to come and talk to him. Instead, I said a breezy "See you later" and left.

Further Note to the Above: Cut and Run doesn't always work. The problems follow you around until you take care of them.

It was snowing like crazy outside, or rather like Christmas Eve. D and D were using matching red shovels to clear their sidewalk—by throwing snow on *our* sidewalk. But what the heck, it was Christmas Eve, and Hugo could clear ours this evening. I shivered in my coat and wished I'd put on a hat or at least gloves. But there was that darn cool rule.

Cool Rule: The colder you are, the cooler you are. As in appearance and attitude. Dumb, huh? But hey, I don't make the cool rules. I just follow them. I wonder who does make them? Probably someone wrapped in a parka!

I paced up and down the sidewalk in front of Biff's house

rehearsing what I'd say. Truth? I was scared. What if Biff didn't ever want to be my friend again? I wrapped my arms around myself to stop shivering. If I didn't do something soon, Biff would find an ice sculpture of a terrified girl on her sidewalk. As I rehearsed yet another way to apologize, Biff's front door opened.

"Are you going to stand out there forever, you *hamar*?"

That's when I knew she'd forgiven me. I hugged Biff right there on the doorstep, in full view of everyone, not even caring if people thought we were lesbians.

Biff agreed, as I knew she would, that I'd been a total idiot, but said she understood about peer pressure, as she was not immune to it herself, and that the teen years were a time of turbulence and journeying toward self-discovery and that every culture on earth had the same challenges and rites of passage. (Don't you just love her? I sure do.) Then she admitted that she *had* been a tiny bit jealous of my new popularity (I knew it!), and that she herself had difficulty talking to boys.

"Seriously?" I said. "But you're gorgeous. Boys love you. Oh, wait. Is that why you wear glasses?" I asked. "So you don't have boys hitting on you all the time and you having to talk to them?"

"You know, T, that's very insightful. That could very well be what is holding me back."

And I felt just like I'd completed Psychology 101.

I told her that Greg had begged (okay, slight exaggeration) to be my boyfriend again, but I had turned him down. "I don't want to have a boyfriend right now," I said.

Then, after I took a deep breath: "I know you want to go out with A..." No, I wasn't to think of him like that anymore. Especially if he was going to be Biff's boyfriend. "With Adam," I continued. "And that's okay with me."

"Adam's cute," Biff said. "But I don't want to go out with him. We're just friends."

"But that day at my locker you were together," I began.

"We were coming to tell you to ignore all the stuff that had been going on. Adam felt really bad that Greg had told everyone and we wanted to let you know you had our support. I would have said something, but well, after you turned on Talia like that, I didn't feel I knew you anymore."

"I know. I've been a complete jerk. I e-mailed Talia and apologized. Did you know that was her name? Talia? Anyway," I went on. "I asked her if she wanted to get together next week, but she hasn't gotten back to me yet. You know, she sent me an e-mail asking about Nannu."

Biff looked embarrassed. "I'm sorry I never asked you about Nannu. That was awful of me. How is he?"

I started to cry. I had missed her so much. It took me two hours to tell Biff about Nannu, Mom, Boo-Boo, and my latex allergy (Biff said not to worry, they made non-latex *condiments*, so no convent for me! Though that doesn't mean I'm going to run right out and have sex. I'm not. I'm waiting until the time is right, whenever that is. I hope someone informs me.) I told her all about kissing Greg and the sock falling out of my bra. We rolled all over her bed laughing about that. Then I apologized again.

"I had a serious case of boy-crazies," I told her.

Boy-Crazies: A condition teenage girls suffer from in which exposure to males makes them temporarily insane.

I pulled my coat back on. "I need to finish my Christmas shopping," I said

"Do you have a list of what you need?" Biff asked.

"Of course." I pulled my Christmas shopping list from my pocket.

My Christmas Shopping List:
1. Dad—a gallon of window-washer fluid
2. Mom—a peanut butter chocolate bar
3. Sophia and Anthony—I'll rent them a romantic movie for them to watch together (and remind them to take it back right away so I don't have to pay late charges.)
4. Hugo—sports drink
5. Boo-Boo—a carton of milk which Mom will drink and that will benefit Boo-Boo.

Okay, busted. I'd drawn up a list of gifts that I could get at the corner gas station. I was scared to go to the mall.

"That's a gas station list," Biff said. Our brains were back in best-friend sync. "I'll go with you to the mall."

"I can't go to the mall," I told Biff. "Ashleigh will be out to get me. I think Hugo might have broken a date with her."

"She won't touch you if I'm there," Biff promised. "You can't let her stop you from going places you want to go. That gives her way too much power over you. Show her you're not afraid."

"But I am afraid," I said. "I'm a wimp. A wuss." Finally, "Okay," I reluctantly agreed. "Just keep her away from my face. I don't want another broken nose."

We revamped my list, upgrading the gifts from pathetic to decent, though I still got Hugo a sports drink—along with pucks and a hockey poster. I even bought Boo-Boo a toy that lets you dial up an animal and pull a string to hear that animal's sound. Biff and I had a blast with it, so I knew Boo-Boo would love it. I bought Grandma T an earthenware mug (hopefully she won't put her teeth in it) and Nanna a pasta cookbook. I still couldn't think of a thing to get Nannu.

It was a little nerve-wracking, expecting to be jumped any minute. But the mall was so packed with last-minute Christmas shoppers like ourselves that I doubted Ashleigh could find me anyway, so I began to relax. I crossed off everything on my shopping list, and Biff and I bought each other matching necklaces for our special Christmas gifts.

"I'm also giving a donation to the Alzheimer's Society in Nannu's name," Biff said. "Maybe they'll find a cure really soon."

I hugged her hard.

When I arrived home, I ran my presents upstairs to wrap, then sent a quick e-mail to Phillip, apologizing. I ended it with "YOUR FRIEND" so he wouldn't think I was hitting on him. My Things to Do on Christmas Eve list was complete, except for the one thing that was on the list in my mind, but not written down. Nannu. I was a wimp. A wuss.

Moment of Truth: Nannu's eyes smile on me in a special way, and I feel safe and loved. Now I'm terrified he will look at me like he did in History class, and not know who I am. If he doesn't know who I am, can he still love me?

x is For X-CelleNt
(as in X-cellent Idea!)

Christmas Eve, before Midnight Mass. I was sitting on my own bed with Barbie and Ken. Grandma T didn't mind if I used my room, even though it was temporarily hers. She said she knew about needing time for oneself and that she appreciated my giving up my room while she stayed with us. And I did need time alone, because I was desperate. I could not think of a great gift for Nannu. Ordinary stuff wouldn't do. It had to be brilliant, stupendous, the best gift anyone had ever given anyone else in the entire history of the world. (Except, of course, for the gift of Jesus.)

I balled up a sock (gee, they're useful) and pushed it under Barbie's dress to make her pregnant. Very appropriate for Christmas Eve, I thought, what with it being the celebration of Mary and Joseph and the babe. Except Ken wasn't seeing it that way.

Ken: Latex allergy? What latex allergy?
Barbie: I told you all about it, but your head was too full of thoughts of plastic brains to hear.
Ken: Latex allergy?
Barbie: It's too late now, so quit whining.

I left the two of them to sort it while I went to church. Maybe there I would get some heavenly intervention and think of a gift for Nannu.

Now, Christmas Day is great because you get all this cool STUFF, but I like Christmas Eve better, because that's when you get family. What I mean is that on Christmas Day everyone opens their gifts then drifts away to examine the loot on their own. Sophia goes over to Anthony's and later in the day we go to Aunt Grace's. But on Christmas Eve, there's no loot standing between us. We're all together. Even Grandma T (a die-hard Methodist) decided to come to Midnight Mass with us this year.

Hugo tried to freak her out and told her that at Mass, a lamb is sacrificed at the front of the church. Grandma T said that perhaps this year they would revise that tradition and have a human sacrifice instead, and looked directly at Hugo. I think being around us has rubbed off on Grandma T and made her cool.

Candlelight softened the shadows in the upper reaches of the church, and the scent of incense tickled my nose.

The place was packed. We were all there—Mom and Dad, Grandma T, Nannu and Nanna, Sophia and Anthony, Hugo and I. Pretty much like every Christmas Eve Mass I could remember.

Remember!

Omigosh! (In church, you can't say it the other way.) It just came to me! Like a Christmas miracle. I knew what to give Nannu. I almost jumped right out of the pew in my excitement. It was the best gift ever.

It took forever to get home! Dad decided to drive around the neighborhood on the way back to show Grandma T the Christmas lights on the houses, even though I reminded him we had our very own Christmas lights on our very own house, and why couldn't they stand outside and look at those instead of all this driving around? Gas emissions? Global warming?

He ignored me.

Finally we got home and I tore upstairs. "Don't forget to put out the milk and cookies," I yelled over my shoulder to Hugo.

"Santa would rather have beer," Hugo shouted back.

"They are such children," I heard Sophia say to Anthony. "Honestly, still putting out chocolate chip cookies for Santa."

"Yeah, what he really likes are nachos," Dad said.

I went into my room and tossed out all the clothes from the bottom of my closet. Searching. Searching. There it was. A blank scrapbook that Grandma T had given me last year (at the time I'd thought it was a lame gift, so I'd buried it in the back of my closet.) Scrapbook in hand, I ran back downstairs and into the dining room. I pushed aside some of the brunch dishes that were set for tomorrow and placed the scrapbook on the table. In the living room, I pulled out all the photo albums from the wall unit and got to work on Nannu's gift.

At one point Mom came in, glanced at the pile of photographs I'd pulled from albums, and kissed the top of my head. "Don't stay up too late," she said.

"I won't. Night, Mom. Night, Boo-Boo."

I heard Anthony leave a little later, and Dad munching on the nachos we'd put out for Santa. Then the house grew quiet around me.

I worked steadily but it was a big job, sorting and choosing just the right thing. I'd have to stay up all night to get it done before tomorrow. Grandma T came into the dining room with a cup of hot chocolate for me. I stole a glance at her before I sipped, but her teeth were still in her mouth.

"Would you like some help? How about if you choose, and I arrange them for you?" Grandma T offered.

I thought for a moment. It was *my* present for Nannu, but I didn't think he'd mind if Grandma T helped.

We worked silently for half an hour.

"I see your doll is expecting," Grandma T suddenly said.

Oops, I'd left Pregnant Barbie out.

"Yeah. But it's okay. I married her and Ken last week," I assured her.

"Oh well, then. It is entirely proper," she said.

"Entirely," I repeated.

"Totally," she added after a moment.

Startled, I looked up and saw Grandma smiling as she glued another picture into the scrapbook.

"I was really scared at the school, you know," I said a few minutes later. "I mean, when Nannu didn't know me."

"It was frightening for me too," Grandma T said. "When I was a little girl and sent away during the war, it was so different and so sudden, it felt as if someone had dug a hole all around me and I was teetering on the edge. It felt as though I had no solid ground around me anymore. That's what happens when your life changes suddenly."

"That's exactly how I feel!" I couldn't believe Grandma T had felt like that too.

"Everyone feels that way at sometime or other," Grandma T said. "But always remember that you have a family who loves you and can be with you through the hard times. It helps a lot."

"I'm glad you were there that day in History class," I said.

"Thank you," Grandma T said. She flipped a page over. "There are only two pages left in the book. Do you have any more pictures?"

"I want to leave those blank," I told her.

I looked over Nannu's present as Grandma T put away the photo albums.

"Do you think he'll like it?" I asked.

"I am sure he'll love it," Grandma T said.

25

y is For YuLetide

Text Message
8:47 a.m.
December 25
To: Biff
From: T
Subject: Merry, Merry Christmas

> You are getting this message from my new CELL
> PHONE!
> L8R
> T

I can't believe it, but Mom and Dad got me my very own cell phone! They got one for Hugo too. They said they would pay ten dollars a month toward the service, which they thought would be the amount used for emergency and family calls, and we would have to pay for additional phone minutes. Luxury, not a necessity—blah, blah. And the phone came with some rules, like I can't use it or the text-messaging in school. But I can live with that!

"What about the brain damage?" Hugo asked.

Note to the Uninformed or Dumb Like Hugo: Never remind your parents of their past objections when they finally give in. They might change their minds!!

Grandma T gave me a funky hat, with a scarf and mittens to match. I could actually even wear them. When I opened her gift, she said, "Perhaps you can begin a fashion trend in which it is cool to be warm and not catch your death of cold."

Along with his *heart gifts*, Hugo also gave me some magazines. Turns out he shoveled some of our neighbors' driveways and earned a bit of money—at Dad's urging when he heard about the *heart gifts* plan (a.k.a. the cheap person's plan).

I realized, once everyone had opened their gifts from Hugo—Dad got window-washer fluid, Sophia got a snow-brush, Mom got two chocolate bars—that *he* had done his shopping at the gas station! No mall for him.

Sophia gave me two new bras and matching thongs.

"They're slightly padded with foam this time," she said, as I held up the bras.

No more embarrassing moments.

Dad picked up one of the thongs, twirled it around his finger, and stretched it back like a sling-shot. "What the heck is this thing?" he asked.

"Women's underwear," Sophia told him.

Dad dropped it like a hot carrot. (Nannu's saying.)

At that point Mom got all teary. "This is the last Christmas we'll have together as a family," she said. "Next year Sophia will be married and off on her own."

"Yeah, but we'll have Boo-Boo to take her place," Hugo reminded her. "We won't even know Sophia is gone."

Dad intervened before Sophia (TWWC) could take down Hugo. "Time to get ready to go to Aunt Grace's," he announced happily, looking forward to his beer and television.

I went upstairs to get dressed, taking my cell phone with me. (Why hadn't it rung yet? No one had called me!) Grandma T had her suitcase packed and by the front door, and I had my room back to myself. Pregnant Barbie and Ken sat on the night table next to my bed.

Fake Thought: I'm so GLAD to be in my own room. No more Sophia!

Real Thought: I'm really going to miss having Sophia here. She's my big sister!

The fake thought was to distract me from the real thought, in case I cried. I felt like crying all the time lately. I wasn't pregnant, so it couldn't be hormones.

I pulled the sock out from under Barbie's dress. "Congratulations," I said. "It's a sock."

I put Barbie and Ken on my pillow and sat crossed-legged in front of them. "It's time we talked," I began. "Life is all about change. I'll be fifteen in six days. Sophia is getting married in less than two months, and there will be a new baby in the family in the spring. Biff is my best friend again, and I have a cell phone—though I don't understand why no one has called me yet. It's not that I don't appreciate all you have done for me—the advice, the lists, the role-playing—but I think it's time we went our separate ways. I'll always be around if you need me."

With that, I placed Barbie and Ken into the top drawer of my dresser and gently laid my old flat bra over the top of them. I bowed my head for a brief moment, then realized they weren't dead and I didn't need a funeral. They were just resting, until Boo-Boo was old enough to play with them.

• • • • •

Aunt Grace's walls bulged with family. Two tables had been joined together, stretching out from the dining room to run the length of the living room. Four of my female cousins were setting plates and cutlery and wine glasses on it. Hugo had immediately rounded up some of the younger cousins for a game of street hockey, and I could hear them shouting outside. Dad sat in the family room with my uncles with a beer in his hand, happy because no one needed, wanted, or expected him to say anything. Whenever one of my uncles said, "So that baby's coming soon," Dad would raise his glass in response and they'd all take a drink. That was all that was required of him.

Nannu sat in the family room too, in a chair in a corner, a blanket over his legs. He looked shrunken. More like a gnome than ever, though not a very happy one. Mom said that he'd had to give up his driver's license, and ever since then he'd become old. Nannu loved driving.

I averted my eyes from him, and went right into the kitchen and found a salad to toss. True, it had already been tossed, but hey, you can't toss a salad too much. Mom shot a glance my way and raised her eyebrows, tilting her head toward the family room. I got very involved with my salad tossing, pretending not to see her. I couldn't stand seeing Nannu like this and I didn't know what to do. I also hated being in the kitchen, I suddenly realized. This was where Nannu usually was, in the thick of things, teasing the women and dancing Nanna around, breaking dishes and knocking food off counters. It felt empty. I blinked away tears—must be onions in the salad.

Sophia arrived with Anthony in tow and soon had her court set up.

Sophia's Court: Sophia is Queen. All the other females are minions who surround her and are expected to hang on to her every word about wedding, wedding, wedding.

I was actually willing to be one of the minions today, because that way I could avoid Nannu.

Christmas dinner was the usual chaotic, noisy affair. I mean, you can't have thirty-plus people in a room and not have some chatter. Surprisingly, Grandma T seemed oblivious to all the improper behavior, including the paper plates rather than real ones. (Keeps the cleanup to a minimum so we can get to the important part of the event— the presents under the tree.) Like the rest of us, she put on her paper hat, blew her noisemaker, and had a "small glass of wine, please."

Nannu sat at the head of the table as usual, but he didn't laugh, talk, tease, or even wear his paper hat. He pushed food around on his plate, but didn't eat much. I caught Mom wiping her eyes once or twice. "Hormones," she told her sisters.

I gripped my cell phone hard, but even that didn't comfort me.

After dinner we gathered around Aunt Grace's silver fake tree. She thought it was beautiful and none of us had the heart (or gonads) to tell her it was hideous. I didn't care. It was what was underneath that I was interested in. Except, this year, I was more interested what I was giving than what I was getting.

Mom had told everyone about the cell phone she and Dad were giving me, so I got enough minutes to last me a year—well, maybe six months (I expect to use the phone a lot). Finally, there was just one present left under the tree—mine to Nannu.

My heart pounded. What if he didn't like it? Grandma T nodded encouragingly as I picked it up and took it over to Nannu, who was once again in his corner chair, an afghan over his knees.

"I made this for you." I put it in his hands.

He opened it and began to turn the pages.

"It's a memory book," I said. "I put in all kinds of pictures of our family so you won't forget us."

All at once Nannu began to laugh. He pointed to a picture of me at two years old with an ice cream bowl upturned on my head. "I remember that," he said.

"You do? You remember it?"

"Sure." He kept turning pages and laughing.

Everyone was quiet, watching him anxiously. I knew they were trying to figure out how much he could remember, but it was making me nervous. Mom must have noticed because she suddenly said, "How about some tea and coffee?" She got up and went into the kitchen, and Nanna and the aunts followed. Soon everyone was busy chatting to each other, leaving Nannu and me alone.

"I'm sorry I haven't come to see you or talk to you," I said softly. "I was afraid you wouldn't know who I was, and I couldn't stand that."

Nannu squeezed my hand.

"I thought this book might help you keep remembering me."

"*Namata*. Sweetheart. Even if it happen I forget your face, I'll never forget that I love you. That's here." He pointed to his chest. "It's my brain that forget. Not my heart. It never forget."

I hugged him hard, not sure if I was laughing or crying. Okay, I was doing both.

He kissed the palm of my hand, and folded my fingers over it. "And that is for you to have for always. I give it to you now in case I forget to give it later. A gift so you always remember *me*."

"I could never forget you, Nannu."

I held my closed hand to my chest.

"Now let me see this book." He turned more pages, chuckling and pointing at pictures, until he got to the blank pages.

"What about these?" he asked. "What goes here?"

"Oh," I told him. "Those are for all the new memories we're going to make together."

Nannu suddenly swept the blanket from his legs. "Who put this *stupidu* thing on me? Like I a sick person. Maria! Where your pastizzi? No one make pastizzi like my Maria. Maria!" He pulled me with him into the kitchen.

26

Z is For Zealous Zit

Text Message
8:00 a.m.
February 14
To: Biff
From: T
Subject: DO NOT!

> Do not make me laugh today. No gagging when you
> see the puke-green dress. I mean that!
> L8R
> T

O-MI-GAWD! I had a huge zit in the middle of my forehead. Humongous! Sophia's wedding day and my debut as
a bridesmaid and I had the biggest zit of my life!

"I can't be your maid of honor," I announced. I threw myself down on Mom and Dad's bed.

Sophia sat at Mom's vanity table, plucking her eyebrows.

"No one's going to notice," Sophia said. She didn't even stop in her examination of her brows to take a look at my zit!

"Yes, they will. I'll be walking up the aisle. Everyone will be looking at me!"

"No. They'll be looking at me," she said.

"Well, that's just typical Sophia behavior," I said. "It's all about you."

"Hey, I'm the bride here! That's why we're even having this wedding."

Sophia got up from in front of the small table and faced me.

"Girls," Mom warned.

I cringed. Sophia was wearing a slip, not her wedding dress so she could, in theory, still take me down. She reached over behind me, and I squealed.

"Here." She tossed a stick of concealer at me. It had been on Mom's dresser. "Keep it. You'll need it more than me."

"Oh, are you planning to let yourself go once you're married? No more covering up those zits for Anthony?" I said.

Sophia whipped around.

"Sorry, sorry," I shouted over my shoulder as I beat a hasty retreat.

I stood in the shower and let hot water run over me

while I thought about the six weeks since Christmas. It had been eventful.

I turned fifteen on New Year's Eve and I went to a party with Greg—as friends. Dad didn't come in and meet the parents, but Mom did. And yes, this time the parents were there.

And Biff and I finally convinced Talia that we really did want her to go to the movies with us over Christmas break. Turns out that Talia is really funny. Even more than *me*! I passed all my January exams, even Health (which I thought might be in jeopardy because of the banana incident) and Physical Education. I'm now in second term. Oh, and Biff and I put together some money and got Phillip a backpack. It doesn't fix everything, but it's a start. I'm so busy these days that I'm not worried so much about the class system. Let the ANs, Ns, and SNs fall where they may. I don't really care—much.

Nanna said that Nannu looked at the memory book I had made for him every day. He seemed more like his old self. The medication was helping and he was only having occasional memory lapses. I turned and raised my face to the water. He'd already told me to tell "all those boys at the wedding that I dance with granddaughter first."

Yeah, right. Seriously, I'd probably get stuck dancing with my cousins, which was just marginally better than dancing with your brother. Eewww. Forget I even said that.

My stomach was in complete knots. Yes, it was Sophia's wedding day, but I had an integral part in it. Maid of HONOR! What if tripped on the hem of my dress? Or accidentally dropped my flowers? Or fainted? At least if I threw up all over the front of my dress, no one would know! (Puke-green dress—remember?) I snickered at my own joke because, well, it was funny.

Biff and Talia were coming to the wedding. I had caught Sophia in one of her good moments (few and far between as the date of the wedding got closer and she became Psycho Bride on fast-forward), and she'd agreed they could come.

I pulled on one of my new bras and a thong and a slip, and went through to Mom and Dad's room again.

Sophia's wedding gown hung on a hook on the back of the bedroom door—frothy silk and lace, the train gathered up in a bustle to keep it from getting dirty. It would be let down in the church and it was my job, as maid of honor, to make sure the train was spread out behind her before she walked up the aisle. I stroked its silky smoothness. When I got married, my train would be twice as long as this one.

My puke-green dress hung beside it, only it didn't look so pukey anymore. It looked more apple green. Almost pretty.

"Come here." Sophia got up from the chair at the vanity table and I sat down. She curled and sprayed my hair, put tons of goop on my face, and next thing I knew I looked twenty years old, very sophisticated, and very hot. Too bad I was wasting all that hotness on cousins.

Mom carefully lowered the green dress over my made-up face and did up the back. "You look beautiful, Teresa. My girls, all grown up." She dabbed her eyes. "Waterproof mascara," she pointed out.

Sophia, still in her slip, inspected me. "You'll do." She frowned and tugged at Mom's skirt.

"You're not going to make me look any less pregnant," Mom told her. "Not at eight months!"

"Think of it as Boo-Boo being at your wedding too," I said.

"Yeah, I guess she is." Sophia finally smiled, for the first time that day.

Mom and I helped her get her wedding dress on (so many buttons my fingers were numb by the time I'd done them up). I hate to admit it, but she was the most gorgeous bride ever.

Dad, dressed in a tuxedo, came in with the bouquets. He looked quite handsome, and I could see why Mom had married him. He stopped in the doorway and stared at the three of us. Tears welled up in his eyes. "My beautiful girls."

"I hope you have waterproof mascara on," I said to him.

"Picture-taking guy is here," Hugo yelled up the stairs.

"Do you have your speech, Dad?" Sophia asked.

Dad's face paled. Why did Sophia have to remind him? It was going to be interesting, though, to see if he made it through the toast. Hugo and I had a bet as to how much of Dad's speech he'd get through before he fainted. (Dad,

I mean, not Hugo.) I said Dad would get ten words out before he stopped, and Hugo said five. I had upped my words from two, because Mom had made Dad stand in front of all of us and practice.

Mom and Dad left the room, and it was just Sophia and me.

Suddenly I felt very teary myself. I grabbed Sophia and hung on to her for dear life.

"My dress! Don't crease my dress," she shrieked. Then, "Oh, forget the dress." She pulled me to her in a hug. "I'm not going very far, you know," she said. "Our apartment is only twelve blocks away."

"I know." But I couldn't let her go.

"I'll miss you sneaking into my room," she said.

"I'll miss the wrestling matches."

"Oh, we'll still have those."

What Happens at Weddings
1. You smile until your cheeks ache.
2. You giggle with Hugo over the weird people on the "other side" of the family. (That would be Anthony's side.)
3. You walk sedately up the aisle in front of the bride, ignoring, but very appreciative of, the complimentary comments.
4. You also ignore your friend's little waves—I mean, it is a solemn occasion—then struggle to maintain composure when you realize Biff is wearing contact lenses!

5. You realize your feet are killing you halfway down the aisle, and you still have the entire dance to get through.
6. Eight-months-pregnant mothers-of-the-bride smile broadly and ignore snide remarks.
7. You smell like fifty different perfumes and cologne from every aunt, cousin, and uncle bussing your cheek. (The cheek that aches from smiling.)
8. You eat until you nearly burst out of the puke-green dress.
9. You giggle at Dad (the mute) stumbling through a toast to the bride. But, hey, he did it. Neither Hugo nor I won the bet.
10. You sneak champagne with Biff and Talia. Bubbles get up your nose.
11. You dance with a boy "from the other side of the family" and get your feet stepped on.
12. You dance with Biff and your feet don't get stepped on.
13. You dance wildly with Talia and Biff and step on other people's feet.
14. You catch the bouquet (prearranged with your sister so that it comes straight at you!).

Before I knew it, Sophia and Anthony had gone to catch a flight to Malta for their honeymoon. The guests began to drift away. I sat down next to Nanna and Nannu and my normal side of the family.

"You next," Aunt Grace said.

"She's only fifteen," Mom protested. "We get to keep her for awhile yet."

Mom looked exhausted and pale. I saw Nanna and Grandma T studying her, and they bent their heads together to whisper.

I perched myself on Nannu's knee. His arm tightened around my waist.

"Sophia's gone," I said. I felt all sad again. "I don't like things changing."

"Ah, Teresa." Nannu kissed my cheek. "That's what makes life interesting. No one know what happens next." He stood and clapped his hands together. "No more being sad. Life, it too short. Come and dance with me."

He swept me out onto the dance floor. We whirled and twirled, until we suddenly noticed a commotion at the table. Dad had an arm around Mom, and Nanna and Grandma T and the aunts were flapping around her.

"Omigawd!" I grabbed Nannu's arm and shook it excitedly. "I think Boo-Boo's coming!"

grade 10: tHe BesT YeAr oF mY LiFe: NOT

Baby Olivia is crying in her crib in Sophia's old bedroom. After she was born, Nannu and I stood at the nursery window looking at all the babies, and decided ours was the most beautiful. Mind you, it wasn't much of a contest. Newborn babies are quite wrinkly and red and, seriously, not all that attractive—except for Olivia. She's the best baby ever. Noisy, though. I hope Mom gets up soon and feeds her. I need my sleep so that I am fresh for the start of school tomorrow. Grade 11.

Talia, Biff, Phillip and I have arranged (over our cell phones) to meet at the corner of Hincks and Jones streets and walk to school.

So, I don't think Grade 10 was the best year of my life,

because I think Grade 11 *is* going to be the best year of my life.

Nannu's right. Life, it too short.

Let's dance.

About the Author

Barbara Haworth-Attard is a native of Elmira, Ontario, Canada, presently residing in London, Ontario with her family, which includes her cat Hubert. June 1995 saw the publication of her first middle-grade novel, *Dark of the Moon*. Since then she has written thirteen novels in the historical fiction, fantasy, and contemporary genres for middle-grade and young adult readers. Barbara is kept busy with school and library visits, conferences, and literary festivals. In her spare time she likes taking walks and eating chocolate candy, cake, fudge, cookies, and ice cream (which is the reason for the walks), playing with her friends (yes, even adults play), and being with her family. Her favorite holiday is Halloween, when clouds race across the orange harvest moon and send shivers up and down her spine.